"Libby!" Sabrina  around this scho~~~ down, acting like you're ~~~

Sabrina knew the words never would have left her lips if it weren't for the absolutely miserable morning she'd had.

Libby stared at her, her mouth hanging open slightly. Sabrina wasn't finished yet, though. "You'd have a different expression on your face . . . if you could put yourself in my place." As she said the word *yourself*, she pointed right at Libby.

At that moment, the air around them swirled. The scene in the Westbridge High lunchroom wavered as if it were a shaky reel of film. In the next instant, the scene solidified again.

Something was wrong. Something was very wrong. But for a moment, Sabrina didn't know what. Then, with a sinking feeling, she looked down at herself. She was wearing Libby's cheerleading outfit.

Sabrina stared at Libby. "Oh no . . . *oh no!*" she gasped. Totally without meaning to, she'd cast a powerful switcheroo spell. She and Libby had changed places . . . and Sabrina had become her own worst enemy!

Sabrina, the Teenage Witch® books

Available from ARCHWAY Paperbacks

Pocket Books/ "Sabrina, The Teenage Witch Space Launch Sweepstakes" Sponsors Official Rules:

1. No Purchase Necessary.

2. Enter by mailing this completed Official Entry Form (no copies allowed) or by mailing a 3" x 5" card with your name and address, daytime telephone number and birthdate to the Pocket Books/ "Sabrina, The Teenage Witch Space Launch Sweepstakes", 1230 Avenue of the Americas, 13th Floor, NY, NY 10020, or to obtain a copy of these rules, write to Pocket Books/ "Sabrina, The Teenage Witch Space Launch Sweepstakes" Rules, 1230 Avenue of the Americas, 13th Floor, NY, NY 10020. Entry forms and rules are available in the back of Archway Paperbacks' Sabrina, The Teenage Witch books: Sabrina's Guide to the Universe (12/99), Millennium Madness (1/00), Switcheroo (3/00), on in-store book displays, and on the web sites SimonSaysKids.com and archicomics.com. Sweepstakes begins December 1, 1999. Entries must be postmarked by April 30, 2000 and received by May 15, 2000. Sponsors are not responsible for lost, late, damaged, stolen, illegible, mutilated, incomplete, postage-due or misdirected or not delivered entries or mail or for typographical errors in the entry form or rules, or for telecommunication system or computer software or hardware errors or data loss. Entries are void if they are in whole or in part illegible, incomplete or damaged. Enter as often as you wish, but each entry must be mailed separately. Winners will be selected at random from all eligible entries received in a drawing to be held on or about May 25, 2000. The grand-prize winner must be available to travel during the months of September and October 2000. Winners will be notified by mail. The grand-prize winner will be notified by telephone as well.

3. Prizes: One Grand Prize: A 3-day/2-night trip for three (winner plus a friend and a chaperone, chaperone must be winner's parent or legal guardian) to Florida including round-trip coach/economy airfare from major U.S. or U.K. airport nearest the winner's residence, round-trip ground transportation to and from airport, double-occupancy hotel accommodations and all meals ($35/pounds per person, per day). Prize does not include transfers, gratuities and any other expenses not specifically listed herein. Travel and accommodations subject to availability; certain restrictions apply. Prize also includes a Sabrina, The Teenage Witch CD-ROM (approx. retail value $29.99) from Havas/SSI, a Sabrina, The Teenage Witch Hand Held Game (approx. retail value $14.99) from Tiger Electronics, and a Sabrina, The Teenage Witch Diary Kit (approx. retail value $16.99) from Pastime. (approx. total retail value of prize package $3,000.00 for travel within the U.S. & Canada; £4,000 for travel from the U.K.) Alternate grand prize: In the event that the grand prize is unavailable, the following prize will be substituted: An Overnight Group Adventure at Apollo/Saturn V Center for three (winner plus friend and a parent or legal guardian). Winner and group will sleep under the Apollo/Saturn V rocket after an evening of space-related activities, including a Kennedy Space Center Visitor Complex group bus tour, pizza party dinner, a visit with Robot Scouts, hands-on activities. Winner and group will get a special NASA briefing of upcoming launches, demonstrations of Newton's Laws of Motion, midnight snack, breakfast and 3-D IMAX film. Prize includes a commemorative certificate for each group and patch for each participant. If winner cannot take the trip on the specified date, the prize may be forfeited and an alternate winner may be selected.
Ten 1st Prizes: A Sabrina, The Teenage Witch Library (approx. retail value $150.00) from Archway Paperbacks published by Pocket Books. Twenty 2nd Prizes: A Sabrina, The Teenage Witch Gift Package including Hand Held Game (approx. retail value $14.99) from Tiger Electronics, Diary Kit (approx. retail value $16.99) from Pastime, Sabrina, The Teenage Witch CD-ROM (approx. retail value $29.99) from Havas/SSI. (approx. total retail value of prize package: $62.00). Fifty 3rd Prizes: A one-year Sabrina comic books subscription (approx. retail value $23.00) from Archie Comics and a Sabrina, The Teenage Witch Diary Kit (approx. retail value $16.99) from Pastime (approx. total retail value of prize package $39.99). The Grand Prize must be taken on the date specified by sponsors.

4. The sweepstakes is open to legal residents of the U.S., U.K. and Canada (excluding Quebec) ages 8-14 as of April 30, 2000, except as set forth below. Proof of age is required to claim prize. Prizes will be awarded to the winner's parent or legal guardian. Void in Puerto Rico and wherever prohibited or restricted by law. All federal, state and local laws apply. Viacom International, Archie Comic Publications Inc., and the Kennedy Space Center Visitor Complex, their respective officers, directors, shareholders, employees, suppliers, parent companies, subsidiaries, affiliates, agencies, sponsors, participating retailers, and persons connected with the use, marketing or conduct of this sweepstakes are not eligible. Family members living in the same household as any of the individuals referred to in the preceding sentence are not eligible.

5. One prize per person or household. Prizes are not transferable and may not be substituted except by sponsors, in the event of prize unavailability, in which case the alternate grand prize outlined on previous page will be awarded. All prizes will be awarded. The odds of winning a prize depend upon the number of eligible entries received.

6. If a winner is a Canadian resident, then he/she must correctly answer a skill-based question administered by mail.

7. All expenses on receipt and use of prize including federal, state and local taxes are the sole responsibility of the winners. Winners will be notified by mail. Winners may be required to execute and return an Affidavit of Eligibility and Publicity Release and all other legal documents which the sweepstakes sponsors may require (including a W-9 tax form) within 15 days of attempted notification or an alternate winner will be selected. The grand-prize winner's travel companions will be required to execute a liability release form prior to ticketing.

8. Winners or winners' parents on winners' behalf agree to allow use of their names, photographs, likenesses, and entries for any advertising, promotion and publicity purposes without further compensation to or permission from the entrants, except where prohibited by law.

9. Winners and winners' parents or legal guardians, as applicable, agree that Viacom International, Inc., Archie Comic Publications Inc., and the Kennedy Space Center Visitor Complex, and their respective officers, directors, shareholders, employees, suppliers, parent companies, subsidiaries, affiliates, agencies, sponsors, participating retailers, and persons connected with the use, marketing or conduct of this sweepstakes, shall have no responsibility or liability for injuries, losses or damages of any kind in connection with the collection, acceptance or use of the prizes awarded herein, or from participation in this promotion.

10. By participating in this sweepstakes, entrants agree to be bound by these rules and the decisions of the judges and sweepstakes sponsors, which are final in all matters relating to the sweepstakes. Failure to comply with the Official Rules may result in a disqualification of your entry and prohibition of any further participation in this sweepstakes.

11. The first names of major prize winners will be posted at SimonSays.com and archicomics.com (after May 31, 2000) or may be obtained by sending a stamped, self-addressed envelope to Prize Winners, Pocket Books "Sabrina, The Teenage Witch Space Launch Sweepstakes", 1230 Avenue of the Americas, 13th Floor, NY, NY 10020.

Switcheroo

Margot Batrae

Based on Characters Appearing in Archie Comics

**And based upon the television series
Sabrina, The Teenage Witch
Created for television by Nell Scovell
Developed for television by Jonathan Schmock**

AN ARCHWAY PAPERBACK
Published by POCKET BOOKS
New York   London   Toronto   Sydney   Singapore

AN ARCHWAY PAPERBACK *Original*

An Archway Paperback published by
POCKET BOOKS, a division of Simon & Schuster Inc.
1230 Avenue of the Americas, New York, NY 10020

ISBN: 0-671-04067-7

First Archway Paperback printing March 2000

10 9 8 7 6 5 4 3 2 1

This book is dedicated to the reader. May it inspire you to do good deeds, like Sabrina does in this story, on a daily basis.

Switcheroo

Chapter 1

"Late, late, late," Sabrina Spellman murmured to herself.

She searched madly through stacks of paper piled on her desk. Nowhere. Her article for the school newspaper seemed to have disappeared as if by magic. And today was Friday, deadline day, so if she didn't get it in, there'd be a huge hole right in the center of the front page.

She lifted up the edge of her purple bedspread and peered under the bed for the dozenth time. She checked the wicker garbage pail, in case it had accidentally fallen in. She jerked open the door to her closet and tossed out shoes and sweaters and dirty laundry, knowing there was no way she'd put the article in there when she'd finished it late last night. She glanced at the clock on her bed stand. It glared at her with its bright red digits: 7:59.

"Darn!" Sabrina said, twisting a lock of her blond hair in frustration.

Her blue eyes stared around the room wildly. She was sure she'd placed the article right on top of her notebook, along with her chemistry textbook. There was the chemistry book, but the article was gone. And if she didn't find it in a minute and a half, she'd miss the school bus. She thought about casting a "find it" spell, but those usually took a while and time was the one thing she didn't have right now.

"Looking for something?"

It was Salem, Sabrina's cat. The fact that Salem could talk wasn't the only unusual thing about him. Actually, once upon a time, he'd been a powerful and charismatic warlock, but after an unsuccessful attempt to take over the world, the Witches' Council had sentenced him to one hundred years of cat-hood. He wasn't your normal house pet.

But then, the Spellman household wasn't your normal home. For one thing, Sabrina lived not with her parents but with her two aunts. Aunt Hilda and Aunt Zelda were witches. When she'd found out about it on her sixteenth birthday, it had seemed strange and impossible—until then, Sabrina had thought her aunts were simply a little eccentric. But now that she'd had time to learn about and understand her own magical powers, it felt totally natural. She loved being a teenage witch! Except for this morning, when she was stuck just like any normal teenager who'd misplaced her homework.

"So what're you looking for?" Salem asked, his almond-shaped yellow eyes staring up at Sabrina from out of a faceful of black fluffy fur.

"My newspaper article!" Sabrina answered, emptying out her knapsack once again to see if the paper hadn't somehow magically appeared in it since the last time she'd checked.

"Uh-oh. It wasn't, like, a stack of white papers sitting on top of your notebook, was it?" the cat asked. He picked something out of his teeth with one claw.

"Great! You found it!" Sabrina turned now, looking at Salem. She noticed something white sticking out of the corner of his mouth.

"Quite a good article, actually," Salem said. "Delicious with Kitty Love Seafood Deelite Dinner." He burped.

"Salem! You didn't eat my article? Tell me you didn't do it."

Salem blinked up at Sabrina. "Okay, I won't tell you," he said.

"Auuuuuugh!" Sabrina moaned. She sank down onto the messy purple folds of her bedspread. "How could you?" She had worked so hard on that article. It was about how the West-bridge boys' sports teams got twice the funding of the girls' teams. It was a story she really thought was important.

Vvvvroooooom! From outside came the sound of a bus zooming by. Sabrina ran to the window and looked out over the budding, early spring trees. She was just in time to see the back of the school bus disappearing around the corner in a cloud of exhaust and dust. *Yap, yap, yap.* The little white dog that her across the street neighbors, the Del Vecchios, kept tied up in their yard barked after the tailpipe.

"The bus! I missed it!" she groaned.

"Hey, I'm really sorry I made a midnight snack of your article," Salem said regretfully. "But you spilled tuna on it last night and I couldn't resist. I'm weak, weak I tell you."

"Salem!" Sabrina warned. She threw him a dirty look.

Salem slunk under the bed, then popped his head out again. "Look, can't you just think of some excuse?" he asked sheepishly.

"The cat ate my article," Sabrina said to herself quietly.

No, Ms. Quick, the faculty advisor for *Westbridge Lantern*, would never believe that one. And she could imagine the other kids' mocking laughter if she ever let those words out of her mouth. It would get around the whole school.

Everyone would make fun of her. Especially Libby Chessler, her archenemy, the worm in the apple that was Westbridge High. And Libby wasn't just Sabrina's worm, she was a worm for anyone who was a little different. Nope, Sabrina could never tell the truth. There was nothing to do but reprint the article. Then she'd molecular transfer herself over to school and be there as the bus drove up.

Sabrina hurried down the stairway to Aunt Zelda's study, taking the steps two at a time. Her aunt's papers were neatly stacked in piles and the labtop—the mini laboratory her aunt used for her work—was folded up on the main desk. On a side desk sat the computer, with a mess of research books Sabrina had used for her article scattered on the surfaces and floor around it. She pointed and the books piled themselves up into a neat stack in the desk. Then, she booted up the computer, pulled up her paper, and hit the print button.

Bleeeep, blattt, cawph, went the machine. A message popped up on the screen. It said, *Error! Cannot print document. I am currently possessed by a computer gremlin. Call the exorcist immediately!*

"Noooo!" Sabrina moaned.

The computer had been just fine the night before. How could a gremlin have gotten in overnight? She didn't have time to figure it out.

Maybe she could reprint the article from the newspaper office at school. She slipped a diskette into the A drive and hit the Save As command. *Bleeeep, blattt, cawph.* "*Error!*" said the computer. "*Cannot copy documents until exorcism is completed.*" Then the font changed on the screen to something curly and gothic-looking. "*Quiet, Minion!*" It was the computer gremlin speaking now, Sabrina realized. "*Submit! Struggle is useless!*" The computer let out some gurgling, laughter-like sounds, then the screen went blank.

"Poor thing!" Sabrina murmured quietly. But sorry as she felt for the computer, she had no time to help it. She'd just have to go to school without her article and think of some way to fill in the page-one space Ms. Quirk and the rest of the *Lantern* staff had saved for her article. The clock in the study said 8:14. She should just be able to spell herself over to school in time for first period. She pointed and, in an instant, she was gone.

But by the time Sabrina's white, square-toed boots touched down in the cleaning supply closet at Westbridge High, it was already 8:30. On her way over to school, she'd gotten caught in a cold air front that had blown her halfway across town and given her a terrible case of the frizzles on top of it. "Ugh!" Sabrina groaned in frustration, running her fingers through her tangled hair. She

6

couldn't go out there looking like this. She could just hear Libby making fun of her, "Hey Sabrina, where'd you get the freaky perm?"

Sabrina stopped herself. She had to get a grip on herself. She was starting to get really stressed out. She looked around—mops and brooms were dangling in her face, the cleaning supplies were stacked on the shelves—and she started to panic. *Focus,* she told herself. *It's not going to help things if I get totally wound up.*

She took a deep breath, then let it out. She smoothed her blue-and-white-striped mini-dress, which had become somewhat wrinkled in transport. She'd meant to change into something different before she'd left the house—this dress had a tendency to make her look as if she'd eaten a whole bag of chocolate chip cookies on her own—but she hadn't had time what with looking for the article and everything. She tugged her white tights back into place. *Pop.* One of her nails burst through the nylon. A long run appeared down her leg.

"Yarrrgh!" Sabrina complained. How come tights always ripped the very first time you wore them? She looked at the run sadly, then whispered a spell. *"Let's turn around this crummy day. Run-in-my-tights, run the other way!"* She pointed and the rip reversed itself, closing up as it ran up her leg, just like a zipper. But when it got to the top, it kept going. A new run opened

7

up. "Stop!" Sabrina cried, but it didn't until it had reached all the way up her thigh and disappeared under her dress. She looked at it, shaking her head. Well, at least nothing else could possibly go wrong.

Rattle, rattle. Uh-oh. Something else was going wrong . . . Sabrina shrunk into the farthest corner of the supply closet, watching as the doorknob turned. The door swung open to reveal . . . Mr. Kraft, the school's vice principal. He glowered at Sabrina through his little round glasses. The light glinted off them, hiding the evil expression Sabrina knew was in his eyes. His sparse brown hair was a mess and it looked as though he'd tried to comb it over a bald spot.

"Sabrina Spellman!" he growled. He stroked his mustache with one hand and grasped a clipboard of detention slips in the other. "Last time I found you in this closet, at least you were in here with a boy! This time . . . well, I can't imagine what you're doing in here alone!"

Sabrina grinned through her teeth. "Well I was just . . ." She couldn't think of a plausible explanation.

But for the first time that morning, she got lucky. Mr. Kraft held up his hand. "No. Don't tell me. I don't want to know the depths to which a teenager can sink! By the way, you're late for first period. That's a big fat detention for you."

He scribbled on a detention slip, ripped it off his clipboard, and handed it to Sabrina with a smile. "Have a nice day," he said. Then he turned and left the supply closet, his shoes squeaking against the linoleum floor.

Sabrina ground her teeth in frustration and stuffed the detention slip into the pocket of her dress. Mr. Kraft's pets never had to stay after school, no matter what they'd done. Jealously, she wondered if Libby Chessler had ever even held a detention slip in her hand. She buried her head in her hands. Things just had to get better today or she was going to end up taking it out on someone.

She sighed, pushed herself to her feet, and slung her knapsack over her shoulder. Then, Sabrina stepped out of the closet, following in Mr. Kraft's path. First period was chemistry class. Her teacher liked her, so she probably wouldn't get yelled at for being late, and at least she wouldn't have to figure out what to do about the newspaper article for another few periods. She hurried to class, the heels of her boots making an echoing sound through the empty hallway. When she got to the classroom, she pushed open the door quietly, very quietly . . .

Keeeerashhhh. Sabrina looked down to find pieces of a model hydrogen molecule scattered all over the floor. Snickers echoed around the room. "Clumsy *and* late," Libby Chessler shouted out.

Sabrina felt like she was about to explode. *I give up,* she thought hopelessly. It was only 8:38 in the morning and already the day had her whipped!

Sabrina stepped into the lunchroom feeling as tense as a stretched rubber band. Crinkled up brown paper bags and plastic trays lay sprawled across the tables. Around her, kids sat at long tables, chattering over sandwiches they'd brought from home or complaining about the school lunch plates of liver surprise and mashed potatoes. A thick, dull smell leaked out of the kitchen. A line of kids curled out from in front of the lunch counter.

Sabrina felt almost timid as she added herself to the end of it. Most days, she looked forward to lunch, when she could sneak a few kisses from her boyfriend, Harvey, or catch up on gossip with her best friend, Val. Sometimes she would just sit there and listen to Gordie chatter on about some science project he was working on that would save the world—or maybe just improve the school lunch. But today, she had a feeling something really awful was going to happen.

She tapped her foot, waiting for the line to move. It didn't. She looked over the tops of the other kids' heads, craning her neck to find Harvey or Val or anyone else she knew, but no one was around. *Fwip,* a dollop of mashed potatoes whizzed through the air and landed smack in the back of Sabrina's head. "Ewww!" she moaned.

She used the last reserves of her energy to comb the stuff out of her hair, stifling the urge to find whoever had thrown the potatoes and force them to eat an entire plate of liver surprise. It wouldn't help to lose her temper—though with each new incident, it was getting harder and harder to control herself. Maybe after school—actually, after detention—she'd go over to the recycling center and ask people to let her throw their bottles into the big metal bin. The sound of breaking glass might actually calm her down in the mood she was in!

"Oooo, nice outfit," came a voice from behind Sabrina.

She turned. Libby Chessler was standing there, flanked by her two best friends, Cee Cee and Jill. The three girls wore identical green and white cheerleader outfits, identical pigtail hair styles and identical self-satisfied smirks. Sabrina let out a huge sigh. Why didn't Libby and her friends find someone else to pick on? She just didn't know if she could take it today.

"I really *do* like your dress," Libby went on, shaking her dark hair, her brown eyes flashing meanly. "Though it sort of makes you look as though you'd eaten a whole bag of chocolate chip cookies on your own."

A few of the kids standing nearby giggled. The others stood back a little, but Sabrina could see them listening in, waiting to see what would happen next. They'd watched Libby go through this routine a thousand times before and they'd probably see her go through it a thousand times again.

"Please, don't start with me," Sabrina said quietly. It took a lot of patience to get through a conversation with Libby, and after the kind of morning Sabrina had, she just didn't have any left.

Libby put on the best imitation of a sweet smile she could muster. "Why, Sabrina, don't get all insulted. We all have our puffy days. Our pig-out days. Our don't-I-just-look-like-a-gigantic-whale days! Last month, maybe I had one. Today, well, it's obviously your turn." Cee Cee made some oinking sounds while Jill snickered meanly.

"Libby . . ." Sabrina said, a warning tone in her voice.

But Libby just ignored it. "Of course, the difference between me on a puffy day and you on a puffy day is that I'm a puffy cheerleader and you're a puffy freak!" She giggled as she said the word "freak."

Urgggghg!

"Libby!" Sabrina snapped, the name firing out of her mouth like a bullet. "You walk around this school putting people down, acting like you're so perfect, like you never had a zit in your life!"

"I *do* have pretty great skin," Libby said, patting her own cheek.

"Yeah, but your personality needs a really strong antibacterial ointment!"

Sabrina had saved up these words after months—years—of needling and nasty comments from Libby and her friends. And she wasn't just getting a personal grudge off her chest. She was sticking up for every other kid in the school who was geeky or nerdy or even just slightly different. Libby had had a ball picking on every one of them. Still, Sabrina knew the words never would have left her lips if it weren't for the absolutely miserable morning she'd had.

The words just rat-tat-tatted out of her. "To be totally honest, it's an incredible drag to be in the same school as you. Or for that matter, the same universe!" Libby stared at her, her mouth hanging open slightly. Cee Cee blinked. Jill frowned. They weren't used to people standing up to them. Sabrina wasn't finished yet, though. "You'd have a different expression on your face . . . if you could put yourself in my place."

13

As she said the word "yourself," she pointed right at Libby.

At that moment, the air around them swirled. The scene in the Westbridge High lunchroom wavered as if it were a shaky reel of film. The kids continued to talk and eat, but the sound of their voices faded out for an instant. In the next instant, the scene solidified again.

Sabrina cocked her head to one side. Something was wrong. Something was very wrong. But for a moment, she didn't know what. Then, with a sinking feeling, she looked down at herself. She was wearing Libby's cheerleading outfit. And when she looked over at Libby, she saw her archenemy was wearing her own blue-and-white striped mini-dress and tights.

"I-I-I know this dress makes me look exactly like a whale," Libby sputtered. "You're absolutely right, Sabrina. I never should have even thought about wearing it."

"Libby! I don't care about your dress!" Sabrina said.

"You're right! Why should someone as important as *you* give even half a thought to someone as invisible at this school as *me?*" She thought a moment. Then she murmured to herself, "Why did I say that?"

Sabrina stared at Libby, a curious expression twisting across her features. In an instant, it hit her. "Oh no . . . *oh no!*" she gasped. She thought over her own words and actions. They came back to her like a nightmare. *"You'd have a different expression on your face . . . if you could put yourself in my place."* The words rhymed. They *rhymed.* Just like a spell. And then, to make things worse, she'd *pointed.* She couldn't deny the horrible truth any longer. Totally without meaning to, she'd cast a powerful switcheroo spell. She and Libby had changed places . . . and Sabrina had become her own worst enemy!

Chapter 2

"Sabrina! Hey Sabrina!" Sabrina turned away from Libby to find Harvey's totally adorable grin staring down at her. He was carrying a brown bag lunch in one hand and a couple of cartons of milk in the other. A lock of brown hair fell down over one of his smiling brown eyes. He placed the milks on the nearest lunch table and slid his arm around Sabrina's waist to give her a squeeze.

"Harvey!" she said, falling into his arms. She stared into his face and smoothed back his soft, dark hair. When she closed her eyes, the whole lunchroom disappeared—the kids eating the world's most gruesome liver, Cee Cee and Jill giggling behind Libby, and most of all, Libby herself, standing there in Sabrina's own blue-

16

and-white dress. For an instant everything felt
thoroughly right.

"Do you want to grab a pizza after I finish
baseball practice? The team's got that statewide
tournament in Lowell this weekend and I want to
spend some time with you before we get on the
bus to go."

"Oh Harvey, I'll really miss you!" Sabrina
complained. "And as much as I'd love to have
pizza, I can't. Mr. Kraft gave me detention."

Harvey laughed. "No he didn't, stop teasing."
He leaned in, nuzzling Sabrina's hair. "Come on.
You can leave cheerleader practice a little early.
After all, it will be our last time to see each other
for a whole weekend."

Sabrina's eyes flew open. "What?!!?" she
gasped.

"I said, 'You can leave cheerleader practice—' "

Sabrina cut in. "But . . . Harvey, I'm not on the
cheerleading squad!"

Harvey held Sabrina at arm's length, peering at
her quizzically. "Of course you are!"

"I'm not!"

"You are! You're the head cheerleader. Just like
you've always been."

Sabrina groaned. No! It couldn't be! She refused to let this happen. She absolutely, positive-
ly *would not* change places with Libby Chessler.
She scratched her stomach a bit. Libby's uniform

17

was itchy, to boot! How could the cheerleaders stand to wear these stupid things?

"So . . . ? What do you say? Pizza?" Harvey blinked down at her as if everything were completely normal.

Darn! She really wanted to spend time with Harvey. But she couldn't because of annoying Mr. Kraft and his endless pad of detention slips. "I told you—I really do have detention."

"And I told you, you don't."

"Harvey! I do!"

"You don't! You *never* get detention."

"That's ridiculous. Of course I do. Everyone does. Except . . ." she thought for a moment . . . *Libby!* Sabrina reached for her pocket to pull out the slip and realized Libby's cheerleading outfit didn't have one.

At the same moment, Libby reached into the pocket of Sabrina's dress—now her own dress—and brought out a detention slip. She stared at it, her mouth open. "Wow!" she said. "This detention slip has my name on it. I've never gotten one of these before!"

For an instant, Sabrina felt like she was going to faint. She reached out to grab the slip—*her* slip—out of Libby's hand. No one liked staying after school, but if it meant getting things back to normal, she was willing to sit in that room every day until the end of the school year.

But her hand never made it to the slip because at

that moment, Mr. Kraft strode through the lunchroom doors. Suddenly, the lunchroom was quiet. Kids kept on eating and talking, but they were obviously all trying to avoid attracting the vice principal's attention. Sabrina wasn't surprised, though, after all the terrible luck she'd been having today, to see him heading right for her.

"Hello Harvey, hello girls," Mr. Kraft said. He positioned himself with his back to Libby and her friends, as if they didn't exist.

Ooops. Now I'm in more trouble, Sabrina thought. Harvey slid his arm out from around her waist and they stood there nervously, waiting to hear what Mr. Kraft had to say.

The vice principal grinned. Usually, that meant extra detention . . . except that, today, there was something different about his smile. Something not quite so . . . evil. "Have you checked the cheerleading equipment lately?" Mr. Kraft was asking.

Who, me? Sabrina thought, staring wildly around the room. But Mr. Kraft was looking right at her.

"We've got a budget surplus, Sabrina." Mr. Kraft looked really excited. "This is a chance to buy a whole set of new pom-poms!"

"Is it really?" Sabrina said, trying not to sound sour. "But the school newspaper desperately needs a new copy machine since the old one blew up last week."

Mr. Kraft let out a belly laugh. "Sabrina! What a kidder! What's more important? Airy, shallow school spirit or substantive reporting and hard-hitting news stories? We all know the answer to that question: *school spirit!* Besides, the newspaper's Libby's problem. Let her copy the articles by hand if it's so important. Monks did it for thousands of years, and if it was good enough for them, it's good enough for our newspaper! Don't worry. I'll just put in that order for the pom-poms."

Sabrina rolled her eyes. "But Mr. Kraft! The newspaper really needs the money more. Or you could spend a little more on the girls' sports teams. Did you know that they get just fifty percent of the funding the boys' teams do?" She quoted the newspaper article Salem had eaten.

But Mr. Kraft wasn't listening. "Sabrina, you're acting strange!"

Sabrina sneaked a look at Harvey. He mouthed the words, "You are!" and shrugged.

Sabrina felt so frustrated she could have cried. She was still in her own body, but she'd switched lives with Libby! And no one had even noticed. No one except . . . she peeked under her eyelashes at Libby. There was a panicked expression in the other girl's eyes and she was breathing funny. Libby knew!

Mr. Kraft turned toward the other girl now, with Cee Cee and Jill standing behind her, suppressing giggles. "As for you, Libby—don't forget about that detention slip I gave you this morning. I certainly haven't." He flicked the piece of paper in her hand, then strode away, ready to dole out detention slips and bad news to the rest of the student body. Libby just stood there staring at the detention slip in her hands.

This is horrible! Sabrina thought. She felt herself panicking, too. She didn't want Libby's life . . . and Libby obviously didn't want hers! She had to reverse this switcheroo spell, and fast.

"So, let's grab a table," Harvey said, craning his neck over the crowded lunchroom, looking for a table.

"Okay. You get a table while I wait on line," Sabrina said. She jerked her head toward the line of kids not so eagerly queuing up for liver surprise.

Harvey turned and stared at her, his head cocked to one side. "Waiting on line? Why? You always bring your lunch."

"No I don't."

"Here we go again—yes, you do!"

Sabrina thought about it. Actually, Libby never did eat the school lunch, seeing as they didn't serve salad and designer water. And come to think of it, that did actually sound a whole lot better than the glop the lunch staff was serving today. She put her hands behind her back and pointed. A brown paper bag appeared in one of them.

"You're right, I do!" Sabrina said. They linked arms again and Harvey steered them toward an empty table.

"Wait! There's Val. Let's go sit with her." Sabrina pointed toward where her best friend was sitting alone at a big, empty table. Val was bent over a sandwich, her long hair hanging down to cover her face as if she were trying to hide from the world. She was looking awfully lonely.

"Why would we want to sit with her?" Harvey asked, still moving toward the empty table.

Sabrina stopped short. *Uh-oh.* The sick feeling was back in the pit of her stomach. "Because . . . she's my friend?" she said, hoping desperately that Harvey would just nod his head and say, "Of course. Everyone knows that."

But he didn't. Instead, he let out a little laugh. "Since when?"

Oh no! It couldn't be. If the switcheroo spell had switched her friends right out from under her, it would just be too awful. "Harvey!" Sabrina insisted. "We're sitting with Val!" She crinkled up the top of her brown paper lunch bag with determination and squeezed past the other tables, moving toward Val.

Harvey shrugged. "Okay! But I'll save a spot at this table, just in case." He put his bag down where there were a few empty seats.

Val didn't look up as Sabrina plopped down in a seat across the table, even though it was impossible not to notice her. For a moment, the tension was so thick that Sabrina felt as though she'd just stepped into the White House's Oval Office for a world peace negotiation. Then she thought, *This is silly. If I just act normally, she will, too.* She leaned her elbow on the table as she unrolled the top of her lunch bag and pulled out a plastic container of salad. She was trying hard to look relaxed. "Hey, Val," she said casually.

Val looked at Sabrina furtively from under her eyebrows. "Sabrina, what are you *doing* here?"

Sabrina nibbled on her bottom lip. She was getting that sinking feeling again. "Um . . . shouldn't I be here?"

"No!" Val hissed. "Why would you want to sit with a *freak?*"

It hurt just hearing the word. Sabrina didn't care all that much when Libby and her friends called her that, but she knew Val did. "Hey," she said. "You shouldn't call yourself a freak. And you shouldn't let anyone else call you one either."

In the next instant, Val did something Sabrina had barely ever seen before. She exploded. "Sabrina Spellman, after all these years, I've finally had enough! How can you, of all people, come over here and say that to me? You, who've called me a freak about a thousand times. A hundred thousand times. A million times! You've got a lot of nerve! And frankly, I don't want to have anything to do with you!" Looking very noble, Val pulled the plastic wrap back over her sandwich, stuffed it back in her brown bag, and moved to another table. Gordie stepped into the lunchroom at that moment and hurried over to sit with her. Her face brightened then and she didn't bother to look back at Sabrina.

Sabrina dropped her head onto the table in front of her. On the one hand, she was proud of Val. If Val—and a dozen others in Westbridge High's less popular circles—could stand up to the real Libby that way, it would certainly show her a thing or two. Unfortunately, Val had used up her last straw on this particular day, when it wasn't the real Libby she was sounding off at. It was just too awful. She'd never call anyone a freak, certainly not Val. But here she was, getting blamed for it. Her best friend hated her. Probably, a lot of people she liked at school did, too!

Sabrina felt like crying. She looked around desperately for Libby, the only person in the school who seemed to understand what was going on. But the other girl was nowhere to be seen. *She must have cut out,* Sabrina thought. That was certainly what she felt like doing herself.

Suddenly, Sabrina felt somebody's arm around her shoulders. She looked up. Harvey! She had never loved him quite so much as she did in that moment. She was just so happy to see a friendly face. He bent his head down and whispered softly in her ear. "That was nice of you to try with her, even if she didn't go for it. I never really understood what you had against her. It seemed as though you two really should have been friends."

Boy, is that ever true! Sabrina thought. This stupid spell had messed up her whole social life. She concentrated on the warmth of his skin through the scratchy material of the cheerleader's uniform, trying to focus on that and block the new, horrible reality that had taken hold of her life.

Harvey gave her a quick kiss, then took the chair next to hers, pulling it close and starting in on his roast beef sandwich. Sabrina was just about to try and get down some of her salad despite the nauseated sensation in her stomach when Cee Cee and Jill came walking over and took the two empty chairs on either side of her and Harvey.

Sabrina sighed and a feeling of exhaustion took over. "What are you two doing here?" she asked. She realized that her words echoed the ones Val had said to her just a few minutes ago.

The two girls giggled. "What a stupid question!" Cee Cee said.

"Yeah," seconded Jill. "We are, like your best friends, you know."

They started right in with the gossip. "Did you hear about Brandon Bradley and Gladys Underwood?" Cee Cee asked.

"You mean Gladys Underwear?" Jill laughed.

"Yeah," Cee Cee chuckled. "Anyway, Brandon went out with her Saturday night. Saw a movie at the mall and stuff. I mean, everybody *saw* them together."

"No! She is such a freak! How could he stand it?"

"Oh, some people are just totally desperate, I guess," Cee Cee giggled meanly.

So this was what Libby and her friends talked about all the time. Just a whole lot of gossip. It was mean and, what was more, it was boring. Sabrina closed her eyes, wishing with every fiber of her being that when she opened them, Cee Cee and Jill would be gone and this whole switcheroo thing would be just a bad nightmare. But of course, when she looked up again, they were still there. Best friends? No chance! But before the switcheroo spell, they'd been Libby's friends. And now, they were hers.

This has got to stop, she thought, *and it has got to stop now!* Well, it shouldn't be too hard, she'd just cast a reverseroo spell to counteract the switcheroo. She thought for a moment, then softly whispered, *"Once, twice, then count up to ten. Reverse this spell—make me me again."* She started counting slowly to ten, after which all she'd have to do was point over her shoulder at Libby and, *zap*, the spell would reverse. But she'd only gotten to seven when Harvey interrupted her. "So, you never answered my question."

Now she'd have to start the reverseroo spell all over again and every time she started it over, she must increase the number count. Sabrina pushed back a little twinge of frustration. But when she peeked over at Harvey and took in his incredibly terrific shoulders, great chest, and gorgeous face, the frustration completely disappeared. "What question was that?" she sighed.

"About sharing a pizza after school."

Pizza with Harvey. It sounded really good. Really good after a day like today. But . . . if she reversed the switcheroo spell right now, she'd have detention again. Then she wouldn't be able to go to the Slicery with Harvey. On the other hand, if she held off with the reverseroo for the rest of the day, she could. Hmm, maybe she'd just have to live with being Libby—at least until after detention was over!

"Sure!" she said, making a decision. She'd have a great time with Harvey. And it would be fun to teach Libby a lesson, too. No one should go through high school without seeing the inside of the detention room at least once!

"Great!" Harvey said. And when she looked into his brown eyes, she knew she'd made the right choice.

"Anyway," Cee Cee was saying to Jill. "After

they left the movie, Brandon and Gladys shared a banana split at the Slicery."

"Eww! Germ city!"

"Yeah! So I guess Brandon is officially a freak now, too. I mean, that stuff is catching. Isn't that right, Sabrina?" Both girls turned toward her.

Sabrina rolled her eyes. "Uh, I guess I see the whole thing a little differently than you two," she said, mustering up as much patience as she could. Was one pizza with Harvey really worth all this? After all, they'd probably shared a hundred pizzas together since they'd started going out. Suddenly, she wasn't so sure about her decision to stay Libby for a day. Oh well. It was only a few hours. She'd just have to live through one lunch period with Cee Cee and Jill as her best friends. She ought to be able to stand that ... shouldn't she?

But as they started in on Brandon and Gladys again, she realized that even one minute was far too long. "Hey you guys, want some gum?" Sabrina asked.

"Yeah."

"Of course," they said.

Sabrina pointed beneath the table and a very unusual pack of gum appeared in her hand. Vise Grip Gum it said on the pack. Her Aunt Vesta had told her about this stuff last time she'd been on a visit to The Other Realm. She passed each of her two new "friends" a stick. They unwrapped the gum and stuffed it into their mouths. "Anyway, maybe we should start calling him Brandon *Bra*-dley now that he's dating Gladys Underwear," Cee Cee said, laughing.

"That's funny, Cee Cee, that's really fu—" But Jill never finished her sentence because the glue in the gum had set. "Mmmph. Mmmmmmpphh," she groaned. Cee Cee struggled to unlock her jaws, too.

Sabrina nibbled on her lip, suppressing a giggle. It wasn't nice, but then, if Cee Cee and Jill hadn't been being so mean she wouldn't have had to do it. After all, the gum would wear off in half an hour or so anyway.

"Hey, can I have a piece?" Harvey asked.

Sabrina caught her breath. No way did she want those lips sealed, not even for half an hour—especially when she wouldn't get to kiss him for a whole weekend. She pointed and the gum disappeared. She held up her empty hands. "None left," she said. "But I can think of better things to do with your mouth, anyway!" She leaned over and kissed him.

Ah, perfect! she thought as a tingle shot up her spine. Thank goodness the switcheroo spell hadn't messed that up!

Chapter 3

"**O**ne, two, three four, Westbridge Scallions got to score!" the girls on the cheerleading team chanted. They waved their arms, pumped their legs, back flipped, front flipped, and, at the very end of the cheer, leaped into the air.

Sabrina was doing her best to keep up but the fact was, as much as she didn't like most of the cheerleaders, they were in darned good shape! Just before she got to the final leap in the air, she cast a little spell. *"It's a stupid wish, I beg your pardon, but make me jump like Michael Jordan,"* she whispered. She pointed and when she jumped, she must have cleared three feet at least.

"Wow!" Alison exclaimed.

"Awesome!" Cee Cee said.

Sabrina was surprised to feel a small, proud

thrill tingle through her at their praise. She didn't care what these girls thought of her—or at least she hadn't until today . . . As they went through the rest of the routine, Sabrina cast little spells here and there—one made her as stretched-out as a yoga master, another gave her the grace of a professional ballet dancer, a third gave her Olympic-level lung capacity. She liked seeing the admiration in the other girls' eyes. *Why?* she wondered. But she didn't think too hard about it, just enjoyed herself.

As the girls took a little break, they flopped down on the grass, stretched their already limber legs or fluffed up their pom-poms. Cee Cee started telling everyone about Brandon Bradley and Gladys Underwood all over again, but by now, she'd expanded the story so much that the couple had been shopping for engagement rings instead of going to the movies and buying a baby name book in the mall book store. So much for that relationship. By the time Cee Cee was finished with them, Brandon and Gladys would be too embarrassed to show up to school on the same day as one another, let alone go out on a second date.

She had to stop this gossip, she just had to. The Vise Grip Gum probably wouldn't work a second time. In fact, she had a feeling Cee Cee and Jill would never chew another stick of gum. She thought and thought as Cee Cee's story about the couple got more and more outrageous. But she couldn't come up with an idea for a spell that would kill this story. Well, sometimes magic wasn't the best solution.

"How about we keep on practicing?" Sabrina asked, getting to her feet and scooping up her pom-poms.

"Sure."

"Okay."

"I guess that's what we're here for!" The girls grabbed up their pom-poms, too, and fell into formation. They went through half a dozen cheers half a dozen times each. It was like a high-energy aerobics class times five. By the time they got to the big finale, Sabrina wasn't sure she could get through it, with or without magic.

"Give me a Double U," Cee Cee shouted, leaping into a split.

"Give me an E," Jill said, following her lead.

"Give me an S," yelled Alison Watanabe sliding to the ground, her legs straddled.

"Give me a . . . rest!" Sabrina said, falling out of line with the other cheerleaders. She hadn't done a split since seventh grade and she wasn't about to try now. She tossed her pom-poms on the grass and rubbed her thighs with her fists.

"Sabrina!" Cee Cee whined. "You're being so *lazy.*"

Sabrina made a face. She was tired, yes, but

frankly, she was more bored. She couldn't believe this clique of girls had totally taken over the school. All they did was gossip and go over the same cheers again and again. Sure, the routines took skill and flexibility to do well—but spectators at Westbridge games had seen the same cheers since . . . well, probably since there'd been a Westbridge team. What was more, everyone on the squad insisted on wearing these horrible uniforms to practice instead of shorts and T-shirts. *Either they wash them every night or they've got a whole closetful of these things at home,* Sabrina thought.

"Let's do it again!" Cee Cee shouted.

Ugh! If Sabrina had to shout the same stupid rhyme all over, she thought she'd go out of her mind! "I've got an idea. Let's make up a new cheer!" she said.

"A new one?" Cee Cee asked.

"Aren't the old ones good enough? Why would we want to do that?" Jill asked.

Sabrina shrugged. "Oh, I don't know. Maybe so that we don't bore ourselves silly for the next hour of practice?" The other girls on the team looked at her blankly. "Like, let's try this one: 'One dollar, two dollars, three dollars, four. Support girls' sports teams—fund them more!' " She punched the air in time to her words.

Cee Cee, Jill, and the others stared at her. Finally, someone said, "I like the old cheer better."

"Me too! Let's do it again."

"Yeah, I'm game!"

Sabrina shook her head. No way was she doing this same routine all over again—not with Harvey and his incredibly inviting lips waiting for her at the Slicery. "Count me out," she said. "I think I tore my hamstring doing that last jump." She rubbed the back of her leg, pretending it ached.

"Sorehead."

"Just because we didn't want to do her cheer!"

But Sabrina didn't care. She waved goodbye, jogging across the football field toward the road. Just before she hit the pavement, she ducked behind a flowering lilac bush. No way was she showing up at the Slicery in this sweaty, smelly, itchy cheerleader's uniform. She pointed and the outfit transformed into a flowing purple sundress. Ooooh, silk!

"Here you go. One pepperoni and pineapple pizza," said Justin Schwartz. He had to shout to be heard over the radio and the customers talking and slurping. He placed a gooey pizza pie on the table in front of Sabrina and Harvey. "And here's your diet cola—your usual, Sabrina!" He stood in front of the table shuffling his feet a little and grinning at her with his perfect teeth. Justin was generally known to have the best smile at Westbridge High.

"Uh, thanks," Sabrina said, sighing and staring at the food. As the smell rose off the pie, she felt a little sick. She wished she could switcheroo it as easily as she had her and Libby's lives. She had no idea how anyone could stand pepperoni and pineapple together. But obviously some people liked it because Harvey was already lifting his first slice off the metal plate, cheese dripping. As for soda, she preferred hers regular. But— she'd been running into this all day—this was Libby's favorite and now, she was stuck with it!

Well, maybe not entirely stuck. She slid a piece of pizza onto her paper plate, then quietly whispered, *"This type of pizza's a gigantic pain. Take off the toppings, make it plain!"* She pointed at her slice and the pepperoni and pineapple blipped into the ozone. She pointed again and the word "diet" faded off the can of soda. She took a big swig. Mmmm, no artificial sweetener in this one!

Well, that greatly improved this pizza date. It was amazing how much she'd put up with just to spend this little bit of time with Harvey! If she hadn't known she loved him before, she knew now! But she didn't know how much more of being Libby she could take.

She glanced at the purple face of her watch. The orange numbers glowed 4:17. Libby was probably just finishing detention now. She'd give it another fifteen minutes in order to play it safe.

Then, she'd thankfully reverse the spell—because of course, she couldn't reverse it *before* detention was over or Mr. Kraft would punish her next week for missing it.

"Can . . . can I get you anything else?" Justin said, still standing there grinning. His pen was poised eagerly over his little white order book as if there was nothing he wanted more in the entire world than to whip them up another pepperoni and pineapple pizza.

"No, I think we've got everything we need," Sabrina said. She peered at him. He was acting strange. Usually, he just dumped the pizza and took off. Now, he kept hanging around, even when that family of five over at the corner table practically begged him for a second round of sodas or that cute little couple in the booth tried their hardest to get him to drop off their bill.

Maybe . . . maybe he realized what had happened. Maybe he knew about her and Libby and the switcheroo spell. But . . . no, that didn't make sense. No one else had noticed, why should Justin? "Really. We're just fine," Sabrina told him. She wished he'd go take care of the half a dozen customers who were looking at him as hungrily as a girl on her first serious diet.

A look of disappointment swept across Justin's face as he turned to go. "What's with him?" Sabrina whispered to Harvey.

Harvey swallowed a huge, greasy mouthful of

cheese. "Oh, come on! Everyone knows—Justin's got a gigantic crush on you!"

"He does?" Sabrina gasped. "Since when?"

Justin was Westbridge's best basketball guard, he was gorgeous, all six feet, two inches of him, and he was totally sweet to boot. Half the girls in the senior class would have given up telephone calls for a month to get a second look from him. Sabrina might have felt that way herself if she hadn't been so totally in love with Harvey. In fact, the only thing wrong with Justin was that he had this bizarre thing for . . . oh that was it. Of course! Sabrina dropped her forehead into the palm of her hand, slapping her head. Justin was totally in love with Libby, despite her personality. Had been for years. And now that she had taken over Libby's life, he was in love with her!

Harvey chewed down the crust of his first slice and helped himself to another. There was a little splotch of tomato sauce on his T-shirt already and his fingers were greasy with oil. "You know, Sabrina, it's not easy going out with someone when half the guys at school are crazy about her," he confided. "I mean, I know you love me but . . . well, you could have just about anyone at Westbridge High." He leaned in so close she could smell the pepperoni on his breath. Mixed in with it, she smelled something else. Fear.

But it wasn't Harvey's fear. It was her own. What if this stupid spell messed up things with

Harvey? He seemed to be the only thing about her life that she hadn't exchanged with Libby. She'd been wondering about it all day. Why, when they'd switched clothes, friends, after school activities, hadn't Harvey switched, too? Mind you, she wasn't complaining!

She hadn't been able to figure it out, but it was the one thing she was entirely thankful for. *Just imagine,* she'd thought a dozen times, a hundred times, a thousand times already, *if you had to watch Harvey making goo-goo eyes at Libby on top of having to wear that itchy cheerleader's outfit?* But she wasn't going to ask too many questions about why that hadn't happened. She didn't want to hex herself. After a day like today, that seemed all too possible.

Still, she'd feel relieved when things were back to normal. She checked her watch. The face read 4:36. *Great!* she thought. Detention was over. She could safely reverse the switcheroo spell now . . . as soon as she could find Libby, that was. They both had to be present in order to cast the reverseroo.

As if summoned by magic, the door of the Slicery swung open and Libby staggered in. She looked like she'd had as rough a day as Sabrina had. Her hair was a mess and another run had opened up in her tights—or rather, in Sabrina's tights. She looked around, seeming a little frantic. When she spotted Sabrina, she shot her a look of desperation, disgust, and confusion, all mixed up together. Then she started walking toward her.

"Uh, can you give me a moment, Harvey? There's something I've got to take care of," Sabrina said. She pushed herself out of the booth, took a last swig of her soda, and chomped on a piece of leftover crust. She'd never been so grateful to leave behind a pizza pie in her life. In just a few moments, she'd be herself again!

Chapter 4

"What's going on?" Libby whimpered. She grabbed Sabrina by the shoulders and shook her. *"I want my life back.* You've done something. Something really terrible! And if you don't turn it back I'll . . . I'll . . . I'll . . ." She obviously didn't know what to say—her usual threats and nasty comments just didn't work now that she was living Sabrina's life.

"Oh, don't get ants in your underwear," Sabrina said. "Everything's going to be just fine."

"But how?" Libby gasped.

Sabrina didn't intend to reveal to Libby that she was a witch. She was counting on the experience being so bizarre that Libby would think she'd dreamed it or imagined it. And if that didn't work, Sabrina would just cast a hypnotism spell that would make Libby think the whole thing had never happened.

"Look, this isn't a good place to talk," Sabrina said, casting a glance around the crowded pizza parlor. A couple of kids were already looking at them over their pizzas and plates of pasta. "Let's go someplace private." She nodded with her chin toward the little hallway right outside the restrooms.

It was strange how Libby followed her so meekly. It just wasn't like her usual self. They stood in the hallway, Sabrina leaning against the little metal shelf by the telephone, Libby with her back pressed up against the wall between the two bathroom doors. As they stood there, a barrage of upset, angry, confused words poured out of Libby's mouth.

"What's happening, Sabrina? My best friends won't talk to me—Cee Cee actually called me a freak this afternoon! Detention was just awful. They made me read a book and everything! I was so bored—and to think all my friends were having a great time at cheerleading practice without me!"

Sabrina frowned. Wow, reading a book in detention sounded like bliss compared with jumping around in an itchy outfit in the heat, tearing ligaments and getting a sore throat from chanting.

"What's more, Valerie Birkhead now seems to

think she's my very best friend. But she didn't really act like a friend. She just kept yelling at me about some stupid newspaper article I was supposed to write—as if I really care if I ever see another issue of the *Westbridge Lantern* again!"

Sabrina caught her breath. Her article! Libby was getting the heat for the story she hadn't turned in herself! "Well, what did they decide to do? They can't publish the newspaper with an empty space on the front page!"

Libby waved her hand in the air as if this were the most useless conversation in the world. "Oh, they blew up some sports photos and wrote a few paragraphs about how we have the best boys' teams in the state."

"What about the girls' teams?"

Libby scowled. "Who cares about them? In fact, who cares about any of this? Sabrina Spellman, if this is your life, I feel really sorry for you. It's just totally boring!"

Sabrina sighed. "Funny, I was about to say the same thing about yours."

Libby's eyes opened wide and she gasped. "My life boring? You're kidding! I'm head cheerleader, I never get detention, and I've got tons of friends."

"So do I!" Sabrina cut in.

"Yeah, but I have better friends!"

Well, that was debatable. But there was no reason to get into it with Libby. She liked her own life, Libby liked hers. And they both wanted to get things back to normal as quickly as they could. It was probably the first time they'd ever agreed with each other on anything! Okay, so now all she had to so was reverse that spell! Libby didn't have that ability, so it was up to her.

She whispered under her breath, *"Once, twice, count up to twenty. To be rid of this spell, I'd give up plenty!"* She started counting slowly to twenty.

But she'd only gotten to eighteen when Alison Watanabe pushed into the hallway. She was wearing a pink cashmere sweater and red lipstick that clashed slightly with it. "Oh, hey Sabrina. Are you on line for the bathroom?" Alison asked. She squeezed past Libby, ignoring her.

"No. Go on in." Sabrina motioned with her hand. She had always been a little in awe of Alison. Cheerleading was just a sideline for her. Her real claim to fame was that she'd backflipped Westbridge's gymnastics team right into the championships earlier in the year. She knew Alison and Libby weren't really friends, but they were friendly. Every so often, though, she'd notice Alison sitting at Libby's lunch table. It was funny that she hadn't said a word to Libby yet.

Alison pushed open the bathroom door, then stopped and turned around. "Hey listen," she said, looking right at Sabrina. "A few of my friends from the gymnastics team got tickets for the Screaming Broccoli concert tonight but Jun-Ling's got a cold. So we've got an extra seat. Want to come?"

Sabrina nibbled on her lower lip. It sounded like fun. Alison and her friends weren't snobs, like Libby and her crowd. They worked hard, got results, and didn't shove it in anyone else's face. But Westbridge was a big school and she'd never gotten to be friends with that crowd. And she'd missed the last Screaming Broccoli concert, which everyone had said was totally over the top.

"Um . . . can I let you know later, Alison?" Sabrina asked. It felt weird pretending to be friends with her. She knew that once she reverseroo-ed the spell, it would be Libby Alison invited to the concert, not her.

"No problem," Alison said with a friendly smile. " 'Bye." She stepped into the bathroom.

" 'Bye," Sabrina said. When the bathroom door had swung shut behind Alison, Sabrina whispered the magic spell again. *"Once, twice, count to thirty. Being Libby makes me feel dirty!"* she said, and quietly began to count: "One . . . two . . . three . . . four . . ."

"Hi there, Sabrina." It was Dave Waitzman, pushing his way into the hall. "Are you using the phone?" He tucked a strand of his longish brown hair beneath his New England Patriots cap.

"No!" Sabrina answered, losing her patience

just slightly. She was never going to reverse this spell if she kept getting interrupted.

"Oh, you know, a bunch of us are getting together for a softball game on Saturday. Why don't you come?"

Hmm. She didn't really have anything else to do. And Dave's crowd was known for their massive softball games. She'd passed by a few times but had never been invited to play before. They always looked so intense, with the ball sailing through the blue sky and everyone congratulating one another if it made it out past the wire fence. It would be fun! They'd laugh, she'd make new friends, she'd show them what a great softball player she was! But . . . once she reversed the switcheroo spell, it would be Libby Dave invited to the game, not her.

A moment of doubt settled in. The Screaming Broccoli concert, the softball game—she could miss them both if she returned to being regular old Sabrina. On the other hand, did she really want to stay being Libby for another whole weekend? It was a hard decision.

"Is it okay if I just show up?" Sabrina asked Dave. She was trying to think of a way to reverse the spell and still be invited to the softball game.

"Well, we're usually pretty organized," Dave said, shrugging his shoulders. "But . . . okay!" He squeezed into the corner were the phone was.

Oh, no, Sabrina thought. *He's going to make a*

phone call. And I won't be able to cast the re-
verseroo spell while he's watching. Before Dave
had a chance to pick up the receiver and drop his
coins in the slot, Sabrina pointed. The phone disappeared. Dave looked around, confused.

"They moved the phone out front," Sabrina
told him.

Dave smiled and nodded. "Oh, okay!" He
squeezed past Sabrina and Libby again and out
of the vestibule. Just before he left he turned and
called to Sabrina, "Hope we see you at the game
on Saturday!"

When they were alone again, Sabrina whispered her spell once more. *"This time I'm count-*
ing up to forty. Being Libby's no big party!" She
began to count yet again.

"Hi Sabrina!" This time, it was Justin. He was
looking down at the ground shyly, kicking the
floor with the toe of one of his basketball sneak-
ers. "I . . . I only have a minute," he said. "I left
all the customers to come and find you." He
threw her one of his killer smiles and she lost
count.

"Uh, hi," Sabrina said shortly. Now she'd have
to start the reverseroo spell all over again.

"What I wanted to say was . . . I mean, I know
you're going out with Harvey and everything . . .
it's just that . . ." Justin was taking an awfully
long time getting to the point. But he was so totally handsome while he was doing it that Sabrina

didn't mind. Finally, he took a deep breath, as if he were forcing the words out. "Well, since the baseball team has the statewide tournament in Lowell this weekend and Harvey will be away, I thought . . . well, I thought you might be . . . lonely or something. And that maybe . . . maybe you'd come see a movie with me Sunday afternoon. It wouldn't be a date or anything!" He hurried to add, throwing a glance toward the main part of the restaurant, where Harvey was still waiting for her. "Just, you know, a friendly thing."

Sabrina caught her breath. She couldn't do that! Harvey would understand but . . . he'd be jealous anyway. Besides, in about a minute and a half, she was going to reverse the switcheroo spell and then Justin wouldn't want to go with her to the movies, he'd want to go with Libby.

Sabrina turned toward Libby, who was impatiently shifting her weight from one leg to the other and rolling her eyes. Well, she could understand why Libby was so anxious to get back to her life, with people asking her to concerts and softball games and friendly movie dates. In fact, at this particular moment, Sabrina didn't feel all that eager to get back to her own life. It wasn't that she wanted to stay Libby forever—that would be a terrible fate. But these few fun things she wouldn't get to experience if she switched their lives back right now—those she was definitely interested in doing.

Sabrina turned to Libby. "Hey, what are you doing this weekend?" she asked.

Libby scowled. "Oh, you know . . . stuff."

Sabrina smiled inwardly. Just what she'd thought—Libby was doing absolutely nothing. And once she threw the reverseroo spell, she'd be doing nothing, instead. Usually she had a great social life, but once in awhile there was a dry weekend. Like the one coming up. If she reversed the spell, that was.

If she didn't . . . she looked from Libby to Justin and back again. Did she prefer to stay home and listen to Salem gripe all weekend? Or did she want to go to the movies with Justin— just as a friendly thing? She looked at his sparkling smile. Well, that answer wasn't too hard to figure out.

Sabrina returned her attention to Libby. She was already starting to feel guilty. But was it really such a horrible thing to want to feel what it was like to be the most popular girl in school just for a weekend?

Sabrina made her decision then and there. "Sorry," she said. "The thing we were about to do? It'll just have to wait until Monday." She tossed off an easy grin.

Libby turned so red that her face matched the tomato sauce on a pizza. "You can't possibly mean that!" She stared around her like an animal caught in a trap. When she turned back to

Sabrina, her eyes were filled with fury. "You'll regret this, Sabrina Spellman. This 'friendly date' with Justin? *Everyone's* going to know about it. And I mean everyone! Including Harvey."

For a moment, Sabrina felt frightened. Libby was head and chief of Westbridge High's powerful gossip mill. She could churn up a whole lot of speculation in just a couple of hours. But . . . wait a minute, that was the *old* Libby. The new one wasn't head and chief of anything. In fact, if anyone had her finger on the pulse of Westbridge gossip, it was Sabrina herself. *Yeah!* Sabrina told herself. *Not only are you improving your own social life, you're doing everyone at school a service by knocking out Westbridge's worst blabbermouth.*

She sneaked a peek at Justin. It wasn't only about him anymore, she tried to convince herself. It was about sticking up for everyone who'd ever been called a freak by Libby and her friends. That meant Val and Gordie and . . . and Sabrina herself! It was a human rights issue now. She'd just have to deal with being Libby for another whole weekend. On Monday, she'd knock off that reverseroo spell for sure, no doubt about it. But when Sabrina looked up into Justin Schwartz's gorgeous eyes and sandy blond hair, she knew she wouldn't be suffering too badly. And she couldn't help but feel a little guilty.

More than a little, actually. She wasn't sure what had come over her. Usually, she wouldn't have considered dating anyone but Harvey. Of course, this wasn't a real date, she hurried to tell herself. It was just a friendly thing. That's right. It was just a friendly thing.

Chapter 5

"Your love is like a cup of coffee.
It keeps me going . . .
Even when it's snowing . . ."

Joe Crooner, Screaming Broccoli's lead singer, caressed the microphone stand with his long fingers, his lips practically kissing the wire mesh of the mike. Behind him, under purple lights, Luke Lowlife's fingers massaged throbbing chords out of his guitar, Dingbat Entwhistle pounded out a driving bass line, and Maureen Flicker tattoed the night with the rhythm of her drum kit.

"Wow! This is great!" Sabrina gasped, grabbing onto Alison Watanabe's shoulder in excitement.

Beside Alison, a few of the other members of

the gymnastics team tapped their fingers or moved their shoulders to the beat. Sabrina, on the other hand, could barely stay in her seat, jumping to her feet every time a new song came on then self consciously sitting back down when Alison and her friends remained firmly planted.

Sabrina looked enviously down at an area close to the stage, which a group of tightly packed audience members had taken over as a dance section. It was a mass of whirling bodies and flying hair. Joe Crooner turned toward it now, bending his lean body into the crowd as if he were absorbing their excitement and energy and then spitting it back at them with his song. *"I love you fresh. I love you reheated. I love you double espresso,"* he whispered lusciously into the microphone.

"You know, if we go up front, we can dance!" Sabrina said to Alison. She pointed toward the dancers.

Alison wiggled in her seat but she didn't stand up. "They do look like they're having fun," she said, shouting over the music. She didn't seem too excited about the idea.

Sabrina nodded. "Yeah! And so would we if we went down there!"

Alison tilted her head, sneaking a look at her friends. They were sitting quietly, smiling a bit, nodding in time to the music. "Um . . . you can go down if you want," she told Sabrina.

Sabrina turned her head quickly to look at Alison. Go dance alone? What fun would that be? "Oh come on!" Sabrina said. "We'll have a great time. Screaming Broccoli's music was made to dance to!"

But Alison shook her head no. "We're all pretty worn out from our gymnastics practice," she said. "We're comfortable here." She patted the cushion of her seat.

"Really?" Sabrina couldn't imagine how they could prefer to stay in their seats.

"Yeah. I'm not such a good dancer, anyway," Alison added. "I mean, I'd only look really stupid down there. You go on if you want to."

Sabrina took a deep breath. She knew if she'd been here with Harvey and Val, they'd be down there, sweating in time to Maureen Flicker's drumbeats, no matter how hard a time the coach had given Harvey in baseball practice. Even Gordie would have given the dancing a chance. He might have looked like an idiot but no one would have cared.

But Alison and her friends made the dancing seem . . . inappropriate or something. Or maybe it was that their idea of a good time was just a little different than Sabrina's own. She swallowed hard, then sat down quickly. "Uh, it's okay, Alison. I didn't really want to dance anyway," she said.

If only she could create a double. Then the real

Sabrina could go down and dance while the double sat up here with Alison and her friends, repeating the same three phrases over and over—"Great song!" "I'm having a terrific time." "This is wild!" Alison's crowd probably wouldn't even notice that they were talking to a dummy.

But of course, she wouldn't have a very good time dancing alone. She needed her friends. She missed them. She hadn't really thought about that when she'd accepted Alison's invitation to come hear Screaming Broccoli. She'd figured a concert was a concert, no matter who you went with.

Well, there was no reason to get unhappy about it. This was no record—this was the real Joe Crooner singing his lungs out on the stage. He finished the last lines of "Cappuccino Girlfriend" and the band paused a moment between songs.

"Demolition Doll!" Someone from the audience called out the name of one of the Broccoli's hit songs.

"Depression Is a Four-Letter Word!" someone else shouted.

Sabrina was about to leap up and scream out her own request for "Orange Soda Pop." Then she looked at Alison. She definitely wouldn't approve. But . . . well, what was the point of being a witch if you couldn't have a little harmless fun every so often? She pointed at Joe Crooner. He leaned away from the mike and said something to the band. Luke Lowlife strummed his guitar to life, playing the opening riff of . . . "Orange Soda Pop."

A huge "Yeah!" escaped Sabrina's lips. She quickly looked at Alison and her friends. They were all still smiling politely and tapping their feet. Joe Crooner started singing the first lines— *"Orange soda pop undoes my buttons, orange soda pop leaves me weak . . ."* Sabrina could contain herself no longer. She leaped to her feet and started dancing. It didn't matter any more what Alison and her friends would think.

Thwugg! The ball thudded neatly into the catcher's mitt.

"Strike three!" Cee Cee shouted from the infield.

Sabrina dropped the bat and, head bowed, headed for the sidelines, kicking at the grass as she went. She'd been striking out all day. Libby obviously wasn't as good a softball player as she was. She'd resisted the temptation to use magic to sock one out over the dusty ballfield and past the wire fence. But this was different than cheerleader practice. If she used magic, she could actually change the score and that would be cheating. Sabrina didn't use her powers for that.

She plunked down next to Dave Waitzman on

the bench. "Good try!" he said, adjusting his New England Patriots cap as he watched Jill pick up the bat and take her position at the bag. He'd tied his hair back in a short little ponytail that stuck out from a gap in the back of the hat. "Next time, try holding your bat up," he told Sabrina. "And keep your eye on the ball. Oh, and use a little more follow through when you swing."

Sabrina rolled her eyes. Dave had been bossing her around all day—always in the name of making her a better softball player, of course. She hadn't minded at first but after a while, you'd think he'd realize she wasn't going to hit anything—at least this version of her, who was stuck with all of Libby's skills and lack of skills. But no, he'd kept badgering her.

Thwock! Jill sent the ball reeling out along the first base line. Sammy Martinez caught it at first base and tagged Jill out, but Jim Dougherty had managed to slide home from third. "Hey! Way to go!" Dave shouted, lifting out of his seat. He turned toward Sabrina. "See? That's the way to do it! That's how you win ball games!"

He returned his attention to the field and Sabrina made a face behind his back. Talk about being competitive! Sabrina had thought this was going to be a fun and friendly get together. Instead, Dave was acting as though they were a minor league team with a major league scout sitting in the bleachers.

Sabrina leaned back against the dugout and let her eyes wander lazily over the figures knocking the ball around the field. She thought about how this game would have been if her own friends had been playing it instead of Libby's. Once, Val had swung the bat so hard it had spun her around and she'd fallen right on her fanny. Once she herself had slid out of her shoes stealing second. No one cared who won, not even Harvey, who always took winning seriously when he played football. Sabrina couldn't imagine Dave laughing about any of those things. He just would have been ticked off that Valerie had missed the ball.

Thwick! Jenny Peabody tapped the ball but fouled out. "Aw, come on, Jen! You're hitting like a girl!" Dave shouted.

Sabrina stifled a giggle. She wished she could have laughed out loud, but she'd long ago realized that, with Dave and his friends, there was no giggling allowed. When Dave had asked her to play she'd thought this game was going to be fun—because she'd imagined it the way her own friends would have played it. But now, she was beginning to realize that it wasn't so much what you did, it was who you did it with.

Dave pushed himself out of his seat and scooped up a bat as he swaggered to the plate. He said to Sabrina, "Watch how a real pro does it!" It was his incredibly pushy way of being funny, she realized.

But she wasn't laughing. She closed her eyes. She couldn't wait for this stupid game to be over. She was going to rush home and *beg* Val to go shopping at the mall with her tomorrow. She just had to spend a little time with someone she actually liked or she was going to lose it completely!

"Foul!" someone called as Dave's ball rolled past the foul line.

"No way!" Dave insisted, fighting back. "That ball hit the ground well in bounds!"

"It was foul!"

"Was not!"

Sabrina couldn't stand this "friendly, easygoing" softball game another instant. She pointed and a remote control appeared in her hand. *"I am totally, horribly bore-ed. Make this game go in fast forward!"* She pushed the button on the remote.

"Not foul! Not foul!" Dave squeaked, his voice three octaves higher than usual. He jumped up and down like a crazed cartoon character, finally picked up his bat and knocked the next pitch over the fence. "Yahoo! Yahoo!" he shouted in his mouse voice as he ran around the bases.

Sabrina laughed. The game was much more fun with everyone scooting around like hyperactive chickens!

It was just a "friendly date," but that didn't stop Justin Schwartz from taking Sabrina's hand as they left the movie theater and headed for the Slicery. Sabrina let him take it, feeling incredibly guilty as they kicked along past the locked up mall stores and avoided the eyes of curious friends who poured out of the theater along with them. A few of them pointed. Others whispered.

None of it mattered to Sabrina. It felt good holding Justin's hand—why shouldn't it? He was totally cute, totally smart, and totally nice. But it wasn't fair to Harvey. Besides, what if someone saw them? Once gossip got around Westbridge, it was pretty hard to kill it. On the other hand, it was usually Libby spreading the gossip. And now, Libby was home watching videos by herself. So there wasn't any real danger that people would talk. Yeah, if Sabrina kept telling herself that, maybe she'd start actually believing she was doing a good deed by staying Libby . . . but scratch the surface and she knew she was just being completely selfish.

What had happened to her? She wasn't usually a selfish person. She usually cared about Harvey's feelings. And what about Val? Was she home alone tonight? Sabrina wondered suddenly why she'd jumped at the chance to go out with Justin. It wasn't like her. She just hadn't been feeling like herself ever since she'd become Libby.

Sabrina put the thoughts out of her mind and just enjoyed the feeling of Justin rubbing his thumb along her knuckles. It wasn't a friendly feeling, that was for sure. Part of Sabrina felt like shouting out, saying *"This is all wrong! You're supposed to be out with Libby. And me . . . I'm supposed to be home, thinking about Harvey, feeling melancholy."*

But that part of her wasn't strong enough to block out the other part—the part that was giggling flirtatiously with Justin and snuggling under his strong, warm arm. After pointing herself into about a thousand different outfits earlier in the evening, she'd settled on a flouncy, gauzy flower-print dress that made her feel very feminine, very pretty, and very flirtatious. It wasn't the kind of thing you wore to see a movie with a friend. If she'd been going with Val, it would have been jeans and a T-shirt.

As they moved out of the mall and into the cool, spring evening, the night enveloped them. Away from the prying eyes of gossips, Justin drew her closer. They passed dark houses, and strolled under tall trees. The air felt fresh and light, as gentle as a kiss. Sabrina snuggled a bit more comfortably into the crook of Justin's arm.

"Sabrina, Sabrina," he whispered huskily. "It feels so good to be close to you. I've wanted this for such a long time."

Only since Friday! Sabrina reminded herself. Before that Justin had wanted to be close to Libby. But he didn't know that. And even if she could have, Sabrina didn't particularly feel like enlightening him. *All that matters is my own enjoyment,* Sabrina told herself. *Harvey's off doing his thing, I'm doing mine. That's the way it is!*

The words echoed for a moment in Sabrina's mind and she felt perfectly comfortable, perfectly happy. Then, in an instant, their meaning hit her. *What am I doing?* she demanded of herself. *That's not me talking, it's Libby! I'm even beginning to think like her!*

Did she really want to be here with Justin? When she looked into her heart, the answer was a big, definitive *no!* It wasn't that Justin wasn't sweet. He was. It wasn't that he wasn't good looking—of course he was! But . . . he wasn't Harvey! And it didn't matter that the gossip mill was temporarily out of order because Libby was out of the loop. It didn't matter if Harvey never found out. Sabrina still didn't want to have a way-more-than-friendly date with Justin. She didn't want to flirt with him. She didn't want to hold his hand! She looked down at his fingers, intertwined with her own. She tugged gently but he didn't let go.

There was only one thing to do. Sabrina used her free hand and pointed.

Bzzzz.

"Ouch!" Justin said. He released Sabrina's hand and slapped at a mosquito.

She pointed again. *Bzzzzz.* Justin slapped

again. As Sabrina kept pointing, the mosquitoes kept coming. Each time Justin tried to take her hand, another bug bit him. Sabrina felt bad. Justin was a really nice guy, but he was going to have a whole lot of red lumps and bumps the next day.

I've got to throw the reverseroo! she thought, feeling suddenly desperate. *I've got to do it right this instant!* She knew it as surely as she'd ever known anything in her life. She couldn't stand being Libby another instant. It wasn't that Libby's friends were terrible—some of them were, like Cee Cee and Jill. Others were just . . . well, uptight. Or competitive. Or shallow. Or a million other things Sabrina didn't want her friends to be. And all the concerts and ball games in the world wouldn't make them fun to spend time with.

"Look, Justin," Sabrina said, waving her hand at the fog of mosquitoes that had collected around them. "I . . . I'm not feeling well."

"Oh no!" Justin answered. "Can I get you some aspirin? An ice pack? Chicken soup?" He was all over her again, holding her as if she were a fragile doll that would break.

Sabrina shook her head and slid away from him. "No, no. I just . . . need to get home!"

Justin looked deeply disappointed. He bent his head, avoiding Sabrina's eyes. "Okay," he sighed. "Then I guess I'll drive you home."

But Sabrina shook her head again. "No need for that. I'll get home on my own." She couldn't face a sad, uncomfortable ride with Justin. He was a nice guy. It wasn't his fault that he had a crush on her, it was hers. If she hadn't cast that stupid switcheroo spell, he'd still be madly in love with Libby . . . who didn't have a boyfriend and might have been totally thrilled to see a movie with him. Besides, she didn't have the time to sit in a car with Justin. She'd just molecular transfer herself and be there in a second.

And it wasn't home she was going anyway. It was to Libby's. She was going to reverse that spell before she went to bed that night. She didn't want to wake up as Libby one more morning!

Chapter 6

Sabrina landed on the lawn outside Libby's house and checked out the situation. Libby's blue convertible was sitting alone in the driveway, a solitary dark shape under the glare of a street-lamp. Her parents must be out, and it didn't look as though any of her friends had come over to visit, either. The living room lights were on downstairs and the blue glare of a television glimmered out from behind white lacy curtains. Libby must be tubing out or watching a movie or something. Sabrina almost felt sorry for her. Her social life had obviously totally evaporated once she's stopped being head cheerleader and head gossip at Westbridge High.

It said something good about Sabrina's friends. The spell hadn't tricked them into thinking that

Libby was their friend. But once they'd had a taste of her, they hadn't wanted to spend any time with her.

Sabrina walked up to the door. She lifted her hand to ring the bell. She stopped. *I'm terrified!* She realized in a flash. This wasn't just any old Westbridge student she was dealing with. This was Libby Chessler, the girl who made people's lives miserable just for the fun of it. If she blew this in any way whatsoever, she'd have to transfer to a high school in Outer Mongolia or something.

Just be strong! She told herself. But, as she lifted her hand to the bell again, she realized she'd never be able to go through with this without some help. She pointed and a little bottle appeared in her hand. Confidence Juice it said on the label. Sabrina twisted off the cap and downed the stuff. It tasted like lemonade but it was fizzy, as if someone had added a couple of packets of pop rocks to it. She stifled a burp, shook her head to clear out her thoughts, threw back her shoulders . . . and realized she was ready to face Libby and get rid of the switcheroo spell once and for all.

Brnggggg. Sabrina pushed the bell and waited. Half a minute went by with no sounds from inside the house. *Brngg, brngggggg.* She rang more insistently, holding the bell down obnoxiously.

"Okay, okay, I'm coming!" she heard Libby

saying inside the house. She sounded as if she was in a terrible mood. The door opened and there she was, scowling. She was wearing the blue-and-white mini-dress Sabrina had had on when they'd switcherooed. Her hair was pulled back in a messy ponytail. She was holding a chocolate chip cookie in one hand and there was a dollop of zit cream on one of her cheeks. In other words, she was in total grunge mode.

"Oh, it's you!" she said with a grimace. "I was wondering when you'd show up." She stepped back from the door and motioned Sabrina in.

Sabrina strode over the threshold and down the white carpeted hallway. She followed Libby to the living room, where the TV was blaring something about whiter teeth, fresher breath. A half-empty bag of chocolate chip cookies lay open on a glass coffee table. A couple of fashion magazines were strewn on a lemon yellow leatherette couch. Sabrina plunked herself into a cushy chair that matched the couch. Libby hit the power button on the remote and the TV blipped off. She sank into the couch across from Sabrina. For a moment, the two girls just sat there. Then, Libby opened her mouth and the stream of angry words she'd let loose in the Slicery started up all over again.

"You stole my life!" she wailed. She leaned back in the couch, letting out a groan. "I don't know how you did it! Maybe you hypnotized me.

Maybe you discovered an alternate universe." In her despair, she grabbed a cookie from the bag and munched miserably on it.

Sabrina bit her lip, thinking fast of a believable excuse. "Uh . . . maybe it's all just a very bad dream," she said.

"You can say that again! But if it is, why don't we both just wake up and get back to our own lives?" Libby wailed. A few cookie crumbs dropped on Sabrina's blue-and-white dress.

"Well . . . sometimes a dream seems to take forever, but it's really just a couple of minutes," Sabrina said.

"Okay, okay. Then it's a dream," Libby agreed. "But it doesn't really matter. Dream or no dream, *I want you to turn things back right now!* I can't stand it another minute. Being you, I mean. Having your superfreak life. Staying home Saturday nights, having no friends."

"Hey, I have friends!" Sabrina said.

Libby practically growled. "Oh, you mean that total loser, Val Birkhead? She tried to sit with me at lunch the other day. I told her to bug off. There were a few others, too. I couldn't stand any of them. They're all such freakazoids!" She took another cookie and munched it.

"So you were rude to them. And now you're all alone," Sabrina said.

Libby sighed, licking her fingers. Sabrina had never seen her so miserable. "Yeah, I am." The silence descended again. It didn't last long. Libby took a deep breath and, between cookies, kept going from where she'd left off. "I don't know how you can stand it. Every second is just a total misery. People barely look at me in the hallways. Guys who used to drool all over me just pass me by. One day in detention nearly killed me. And then Ms. Quick actually called me on Saturday morning and made some big fuss about the copy machine in the stupid newspaper office. Said she'd gotten a donation of another used one but that there was no way to get it delivered. And . . . *she cried*. Sabrina, she actually cried about the copy machine! As if anyone but a freak could really care about that idiotic paper!"

"I care about it," Sabrina said. But she realized as she said it that she wasn't really listening to Libby. The *Lantern* seemed very far away now. It was part of a different life, one she felt as though she'd led a long, long time ago, even though it had only been a few days.

But Sabrina didn't have a chance to ponder the feeling because Libby was still talking. "Now *I* know what it's like to be a total freak," she moaned. "And it stinks!"

Sabrina shifted in the chair, its leatherette material sticking to the bare underside of her legs. She was getting angry herself as she listened to Libby totally write off her entire life. A little burst of gas welled up in her—it was the confidence juice. "Listen, Libby," she shot back. "I've had a chance to try out your life and it's not so great, either. In fact, I'd have to say it's pretty lousy! If you think listening to Cee Cee and Jill trash everyone in the whole school is fun, I feel really sorry for you. Cheerleading practice is just a bunch of snobs jumping around in miniskirts so short they show your underpants. And as for all those guys you were talking about— you can only date one at a time, so what's the big deal?"

Libby laughed. "At least I have fun!"

"So do I!" Sabrina responded.

"Yeah! Freak fun!"

Sabrina was about to come back with an insult. Then she stopped herself. Fighting about whose life was better was just completely stupid. They both liked their own lives. Enough said! The real problem was how to get each of them back to those lives. Then, Libby could think Sabrina was a freak and Sabrina could think Libby was a nasty gossip and that would be the end of it.

Sabrina pushed herself out of the chair. "Look, let's not argue. Let's just take care of this problem we both have."

"For once, I'm with you!" Libby said, standing, too.

Sabrina studied Libby for a moment. "You know how sometimes in dreams, really strange, impossible things happen?"

"Yeah," Libby answered. "One time, I dreamed I was driving to school but instead of riding in my convertible, I was on the back of a huge toad. It was really disgusting."

Sabrina nodded. "Yeah, I've had some doozies myself. Anyway, some weird things are about to happen. They're just part of the dream. But they're good things because when you wake up, you'll be you again and I'll be me."

"Great! If that's the case, then the freakier the better!" Libby said.

First, Sabrina pointed at herself. Her gauzy, flower-print dress transformed into Libby's cheerleader outfit. When they switched back, she figured, she'd get her old blue-and-white dress back and Libby would switch into whatever she was wearing. This dress was one of her favorites—she didn't want to lose it to Libby. "Okay." Sabrina took a deep breath. "Are you ready?" she asked.

"Am I ever!" Libby answered.

Sabrina closed her eyes, concentrating hard on the spell. *"Once, twice, count to fifty. Switching back will feel really nifty!"* Slowly, very, very slowly, she counted. By the time she'd reached thirty, Libby was counting along with her. As they reached forty, their excitement began to mount. "Forty-eight . . . forty-nine . . ." the girls said together. *"Fifty!"* As the word burst out of their mouths simultaneously, Sabrina pointed right at Libby. A bit of white lightning crackled from her finger.

"Hey!" Libby protested as the spell hit her.

Sabrina smiled to herself, anticipating the moment. She'd never have to listen to Cee Cee and Jill and their boring gossip again. The next time Screaming Broccoli came through Westbridge, she'd go with Harvey, Val, and Gordie and they'd dance their buns off. She might have to get through a few lonely Saturday nights when Harvey had an away game, but who cared? Hey, she wouldn't even mind getting stuck in detention from now on!

All these thoughts ran through Sabrina's head as if in slow motion. Time slowed down. It stood still.

"Uh . . . so like, when's this switch going to happen?" Libby cut in.

Sabrina's daydream was interrupted and she realized that . . . time actually *had* stood still. Either that or . . . her spell wasn't working. Because nothing had changed. Confused, she looked down at Libby's cheerleader's outfit, waiting for it to transform back into her own mini-dress. She waited some more, scratching at the fabric, she hoped for the last time. But nothing happened.

Oh no. Oh no! Sabrina thought. Something was wrong. The reverseroo spell was a dud!

For an instant, she panicked. She was going to

have to stay Libby forever. She'd be stuck in a life of empty friendships and selfish relationships. She'd have to wear itchy uniforms and act like a creep for the rest of her existence. And since witches had such a long life span, she was going to have to stay that way for a very long time.

Libby looked at Sabrina and giggled.

"What are you laughing about?" Sabrina gasped. She felt close to tears herself.

Libby kept laughing. She spun around in a circle, then dropped onto the sofa, throwing her legs up onto the cushions in one big, relaxed motion. "It's just so funny!"

"It is? How?" Sabrina asked.

"Oh!" Libby gasped, the laughter turning to hiccups now. "It's just such a strange situation. Me being turned into a freak like you—how absurd! Then you coming over and telling me you'll change everything back—as if you're some sort of magician or witch or something."

Sabrina caught her breath, worried. Libby knew. She knew!

But Libby just kept on laughing. "Good thing it's only a nightmare," she giggled. "Guess we'll have to go back to bed and keep on dreaming until we get switched back around."

Sabrina looked at the ceiling, feeling totally stuck. She'd need a lot more than dreams to get herself out of this mess. She'd need strong magic.

Libby continued to talk. "Well, as long as we're stuck in this ridiculous dream together, we might as well make the best of it. Help each other out. Maybe even join forces instead of working against one another."

"I . . . guess that makes good sense," Sabrina said. Now why hadn't she thought of that? It seemed like the kind of thing she would have said, not Libby.

"Here, have a cookie," Libby said. "Chocolate is a good way to get through bad times, even if they are only dreams." She snagged the bag of cookies off the coffee table, took one out, and threw the paper sack toward Sabrina, who caught it with one hand.

Sabrina unrolled the top. It felt funny sharing anything with Libby, who'd made her life so miserable all through high school. But . . . maybe she'd changed just a little. Just the way Sabrina had found herself thinking a bit more like Libby after the switcheroo had sunk in, maybe Libby was finding herself thinking a little more like Sabrina. It could end up being a very good thing, a very good thing indeed. She let her mind wander further. Maybe this experience would totally transform Libby. Maybe she's become a nicer person. She probably still wouldn't be somebody Sabrina wanted for a friend but maybe she'd ruin fewer lives.

Feeling oddly open and friendly toward the

girl who'd tried to make every day at Westbridge High a misery for her, Sabrina reached into the cookie bag. She felt around at the bottom. Nothing, only broken bits and crumbs. Libby laughed as she crunched down the very last cookie of the bag and licked her fingers clean. It was a small thing, but Sabrina hated her for it.

Uggh! Libby Chessler would be a creep no matter who she switched lives with. One thing Sabrina knew for sure—she'd never, ever join forces with that girl!

Chapter 7

"**A**unt Hilda? Aunt Zelda?"

The door slammed shut behind Sabrina. She stood for a moment in the dark living room, listening. The curtains fluttered in the breeze coming through the half-open window. The shadows lay still in the dark room. The only sound she heard was the whooshing of a couple of cars going by outside.

"Anyone home?" she called again. But she could feel the house was empty.

Disappointment curled through her. She really needed to talk to her aunts, tell them everything. They'd tell her how careless she'd been with her magic, how every spell has consequences, some of them not so nice. They'd tell her she needed to learn a lesson. They might make her do all her home chores without magic as punishment. But . . . they'd tell her how to reverse the spell, and that was the important thing! Compared to staying Libby forever, anything her aunts might do to her was about as difficult as being handed a hundred dollar bill and told to spend it on anything you wanted.

"Aunt Zelda! Aunt Hilda!" she called again.

She wandered across the living room and pushed open the door to Aunt Zelda's lab. *"What do you want?"* an angry male voice shouted. But it was only the computer, still inhabited by the gremlin.

Sabrina pulled the door shut quickly and called up the stairs. No one answered. She hurried to the kitchen and stepped inside. It was as empty as the rest of the house. On the high white counter, near the toaster, lay a note. She picked it up and read it.

"Sabrina—I'm at a symposium of women scientists. We're testing out a new car that runs on coffee grounds instead of gasoline. I'm bringing my vacuum cleaner just in case we can't get up the first hill . . . Hilda's on a blind date. Seemed like a nice guy—and the seeing-eye dog was friendly, too. We'll both be back late, so don't bother to wait up. Not too much in the fridge, but point yourself up something healthy. See you later. Love, Aunt Zelda."

Sabrina crumpled up the note and tossed it toward the garbage can. She missed and the balled up paper rolled across the linoleum floor. *How dare they? How dare they!* she thought. How dare her aunts go out just when she needed them most! When Sabrina Spellman needed something, people where were supposed to be there to give it to her! Immediately!

In the next instant, Sabrina stopped herself. What was she thinking! She wasn't angry with her aunts. They were just off having fun, living their own lives. She wondered where that flash of selfishness had come from. It was as though the thoughts had come out of someone else's head—someone she didn't like very much—and popped themselves right into hers.

All of a sudden, she knew. It was Libby! Libby was the one who would be angry and frustrated and downright nasty at not getting her own way immediately. Sabrina felt a nauseated rumbling in her stomach. *No. No!* It couldn't be! She and Libby had exchanged lives, not brains . . .

"Salem!" she called, needing company and distraction. At the moment, even that pain-in-the-neck cat would be better than no one . . . She stopped herself again. Salem wasn't a pain-in-the-neck. She loved him. *Oooo, this is scary,* she thought.

"Salem!" she called again. That was when she noticed the piece of paper sitting next to his dinner bowl. It said:

"Went off to howl at the moon with a couple of the boys. Then we'll head over to the Dumpster behind Captain Nemo's and pig out on fish. And in case you think I'm guilt tripping you about the quality of food around here—I am!"

Sabrina balled up this note, too, and flung it at the garbage can, feeling that same flash of anger she'd felt at her aunts. But she ignored it. She was not switching thoughts with Libby Chessler. She simply refused to let it happen.

Trying to distract herself, she opened the door to the refrigerator. Inside was a half-eaten container of yogurt, half an onion covered with plastic wrap, a white carton of dried up rice left over from the Chinese food they'd ordered out a few nights ago, and a squeeze bottle of chocolate syrup. Boy, Aunt Zelda wasn't kidding when she'd written that there wasn't anything in the house. There was also a small plastic container of wing of bat and lizard lips. *Why is everyone in this house such a fr—* Sabrina stopped the thought before the hated word "freak" could finish forming in her brain. She was not going to allow Libby to invade her head. Still, she had the feeling she better get this spell reversed pretty soon or else . . . well, she didn't want to think about that idea either.

Feeling miserable, Sabrina slid onto one of the

high stools and prepared to point up dinner for herself. What did she want to eat? Something healthy, like Aunt Zelda had said in her note, or . . . *"Abracadabra, fill my tummy with something sweet and gooey and yummy."* She pointed. A huge banana split appeared on the counter in front of her. She went to the fridge, pulled out the chocolate syrup, and squeezed it all over the ice cream.

But even dessert wasn't enough to distract her. *Company, company, company,* she thought. She didn't want to be left alone with her thoughts . . . or Libby's thoughts. Of course, Aunt Louisa! She was always there.

Sabrina turned toward the portrait of her great-aunt, expecting to see the usual painting of the stern, older woman, every hair of her tight bun lying perfectly in place, her lace collar starched and buttoned to the very top, her intricate cameo pin carefully cloaking any last part of her neck that might be exposed. The painting covered up the secret cabinet where her aunts kept their witch ingredients. And when you talked to it, it talked back—but only when it felt like it. Aunt Louisa was kind of a tough old character— though who could blame her. That picture frame wasn't particularly comfortable. But Aunt Louisa was always soft and comforting when Sabrina was in trouble. She needed her now.

The problem was, when Sabrina looked at the

portrait, it wasn't there! In its place was a cheap forgery of the *Mona Lisa.* Hmm, or maybe it was the real one. One thing you had to say about Aunt Louisa—she had a sophisticated appreciation of art. Stuck into the crack between the frame and the painting was a note.

> *"I'm at a lecture on older people in the arts. Whistler's mother is giving it. I just couldn't pass it up! Talk to Mona if you feel like it. She's a pretty nice gal. Love, Aunt Louisa."*

Darn, she was gone, too? Well, Aunt Louisa's company was usually a little flat anyway. But she had to talk to someone. She looked at the *Mona Lisa.* "Hello," she said. The painting didn't say a word, just stared back with that soft, mysterious smile of hers. "Did you have a good trip over from France?" Sabrina knew the *Mona Lisa* was in the Louvre museum in Paris—or was supposed to be, anyway. But the picture still didn't reply. "Oh, a lot of good you are!" Sabrina said, dismissing the painting with the wave of one hand.

She turned her back and hurried toward Aunt Zelda's study. She wanted to listen to the answering machine—even if it meant getting chewed out by the computer gremlin. She pushed open the door.

"What are you doing back again?" the gremlin shouted.

"Oh, be quiet. I'm only looking for a little company," Sabrina answered, stepping into the study.

Suddenly, the computer started sniffling. "Oh, thank goodness somebody understands! I'm so terribly lonely cooped up here in this box all day long!" The gremlin went into a long tirade about how hard its life was, how nobody liked you when you were a gremlin, how, in fact, no one would even talk to you.

"Maybe they would if you didn't shout at everybody!" Sabrina said. "And mess up their computers. And lose their documents."

The computer bleeped a few times as if it were thinking. "You know, you may be right. But then, it's *fun* to shout and make a mess and chew up work people have spent hours working on . . . And another thing—"

But Sabrina had already gone over to the electrical socket and unplugged the computer. It sounded just like Libby and that was one person she was hearing all too much from lately!

She pushed aside a few of Aunt Zelda's file folders that were lying on top of the answering machine and was thrilled to see that the little red light was blinking three times. Great! Maybe Harvey had called. She could really use hearing his familiar, reassuring, loving voice at this moment. Harvey, the only thing about her life that hadn't changed when she'd cast that spell!

She pushed the play button and dropped into Aunt Zelda's swivel work chair to listen. As a high, squeaky voice began to speak, Sabrina felt a twinge of annoyance twist through her. "Zelda! It's Alberta Einstein-Jones. Before you head over to the meeting, could you pick up some coffee filters? We'll need about fifty dozen or so to get the car out of first gear. See you there!" *Beeeeep*.

No Harvey. Sabrina closed her eyes, deciding that her aunt's friend must be a total idiot. *No. No! Don't think that way,* she told herself. It was Libby thinking, not her. She had to hold on to her own mind. She pushed away the thoughts, praying that the next voice she'd hear would be her boyfriend's. But the next sound she heard was a deep voice that definitely wasn't Harvey's.

"Hello Hilda. I got your number from the Desperate Singles Dating Service. Maybe we could get together. It sounds like we have an awful lot in common. For instance, I'm desperate and so are you . . ."

Freak! Sabrina thought. As the horrible word forced its way into her brain, she held her head, pulling at her hair as if she could grab Libby's thoughts and drag them out of her brain. She pushed the fast forward button until she got to the last message. *Harvey, Harvey, Harvey,* she thought. Her stomach felt totally queasy.

Beeeeep went the machine. "This is a message for Salem Saberhagen from Elsie's Pet Shop on Main Street. We got in that special connoisseur blend catnip you ordered. You can pick it up any time."

Darn! Sabrina hit the arm of the chair, feeling frustrated. Just when she needed Harvey, he was too busy playing some stupid game even to call her. Everyone was so selfish, selfish, selfish. They only thought of their own needs, never hers!

After the words had finished reeling through her brain, Sabrina leaned back against the padded back of the chair and groaned heavily. There was no escaping Libby. She was inside her now. She'd just have to distract herself and wait for one of her aunts to get home. But what should she do until then?

She thought about some of the things she usually enjoyed doing. She was in the middle of a really good novel. *Reading's boring,* she thought. She could watch the "Harry Stinger Show," with its celebrity gossip and roster of freaky guests. *That would be fun!* Libby's thoughts said. But the show wasn't on until eight o'clock. She could call Val. *But she's totally a freak,* Libby's thoughts insisted. *And, what's more, she doesn't want to talk to you,* Sabrina's own thoughts added.

But she needed to talk to someone. Sabrina

sighed as she picked up the receiver. She had a bad feeling about calling Val, but she felt compelled to try anyway. She stopped, her finger poised over the buttons. Now why couldn't she remember the number? She'd called it a million times. Oh yes, of course. *Bleep, bleep, bleep.* The phone made the familiar tune as she pushed the buttons.

Blingg. Blingg. Blingg. "Hello?"

A nervous feeling hit Sabrina right in the stomach as she heard Val's voice. What should she say? Val was a good friend . . . who thought she was a gossip and a put-down artist. "Um . . . hi Val. It's . . . it's Sabrina . . ." she fumbled. There was silence on the other end of the line. "You know . . . Sabrina Spellman? I . . . just thought I'd call and say hi. That's okay, isn't it?"

There was a loud sigh on the other end of the phone. "It would be okay . . . if you didn't call me a freak and a loser every time you passed me in the hall at school."

Sabrina sighed sadly. "I wish you'd give me another chance. I've . . . turned over a new leaf. And I really want to be your friend." Even the switcheroo spell hadn't changed that fact—she desperately wanted her relationship with Val to be the way it had been before the spell. No matter what thoughts of Libby's passed through her mind, this thought was lodged deep, deep in her heart.

84

Val listened but Sabrina could tell she hadn't made up her mind to trust her. "Well, I guess we can at least talk," she said. Sabrina's heart thumped happily. But in the next moment, it sank. "Anyway, where did you get my phone number? We're unlisted."

Sabrina licked her lips, trying to think. "I . . . I got it from a friend!"

"Since when do we have friends in common? Who gave you my number?"

"It . . . it was Libby Chessler." The first name she could think of came out of Sabrina's mouth.

Again there was silence. Then, very slowly and sadly, Val said. "Libby. We've been friends ever since I came to Westbridge. But lately, I'm not exactly sure why. You know, the other day she actually called me a freak when I stopped to say hi to Gordie. Then she apologized. Then she called me a freak again. It was bizarre, as though there were two people inside her battling to get out."

"I know the feeling," Sabrina said. Again there was silence.

"So . . . what did you want to talk about?"

Hmm. Sabrina wanted this conversation to be as normal as possible. What did they usually talk about? The newspaper! "Well I . . . I was wondering how things are going at the *Lantern*. What I mean is, maybe I could write a story or two."

Val considered for a moment. "Well . . . I guess

so, but you have to make your deadlines. Libby was supposed to hand in a story about girls' sports on Friday but she didn't do it and now the whole paper looks ridiculous!"

"I'd *never* do that," Sabrina said, knowing that, in fact, she was the one who had!

"Then, there's research. Like, right now, I'm working on a story about how girls' haircuts cost approximately seventeen dollars more than boys' haircuts. So for research, I'm going to all the haircutting places in the area. And I'm sending Gordie to the same ones. We're comparing prices. But the thing is, Gordie's, like, pretty shy. So when they ask him if he wants the haircut right then, he's too embarrassed to say no. So his hair just keeps getting shorter and shorter and shorter . . ." Val giggled.

Sabrina yawned, trying to stay tuned in to what Val was saying. But really, who cared about such a stupid article? And if Gordie was too chicken to say no to the haircutters, he sort of deserved what he got. She didn't want to think these thoughts, they just came to her.

"So," Val was saying. "Do you have any ideas for articles?"

Sabrina tried to think back to the story ideas she'd had before the switcheroo spell. She vaguely remembered something about a food pantry over in Ridgefield. But now, her mind was in a fog. She could only think of stories about cheerleading.

"Uh, listen, I've got to go," Sabrina told Val. She felt as though if she spent another instant on the phone with her former friend, she'd only come up with articles about cheerleaders and how important a role they provide in school.

"Okay then. 'Bye!" Val said. She sounded angry. Or maybe she was hurt. Part of Sabrina felt awful. She'd been kind of rude to Val. The other part, frankly, didn't much care. She hung up the phone, feeling more confused than ever.

Sabrina sat at her aunt's desk, not sure what to do next. The screen of Aunt Zelda's computer gleamed in front of her. Sabrina caught sight of her own reflection in the shiny surface of the monitor. It was her hair, blond and shimmery as ever, her nose, her eyes, her mouth—but with Libby's annoying smirk plastered all over it. *This has to stop. It* has *to stop!* But it couldn't—not until her aunts got home and gave her a hand.

She had to distract herself—she just couldn't face herself anymore. She turned away from the computer and grabbed the phone. Who could she call? Someone less boring than Val. She thought for a moment. She was sorry to realize that she had Cee Cee's telephone number memorized. There it was in her brain circuits, as clear as if she were reading the numbers out of the telephone book. She picked up the receiver, waited for a dial tone, then pressed the number in.

The phone rang once . . . twice. *Click* someone

picked it up. "This is Cee Cee," Cee Cee's voice said.

"Hey, it's me. Sabrina," Sabrina said.

"Hey, hey!" Cee Cee said. "What's the good gossip?" Sabrina stopped. She didn't really have any. Gordie getting a trillion bad haircuts didn't really count. "Come on now. Don't hold back!" But Cee Cee didn't wait for Sabrina to answer. "I've heard some doozies! For instance, Brandon Bradley and Gladys Underwood were fooling around under the bleachers at the last home baseball game!"

"Wow!" Sabrina said.

She wasn't sure she believed it. But if it *were* true, it was a total shocker. Would they really have the nerve to fool around right underneath people's feet like that? What would have happened if someone had looked down and seen them? Well, even if it wasn't true, they'd have to live with it now. Gossip was forever—once a story got out, it was impossible to make people ever completely forget it.

"And then, I heard that Lola Lapocca's getting a nose job."

"Well she needs one. What a shnoz!" Sabrina slapped her hand over her mouth. Had she really said those unkind words?

"And then," Cee Cee shrieked, "There's Libby Chessler!"

Sabrina stopped. Libby. Cee Cee was about to

trash Libby. She wasn't sure she wanted to hear it. On the other hand . . . how could she resist? "Um . . . what about her?" Sabrina asked quickly.

Cee Cee giggled. "She tried to push her way into the Screaming Broccoli concert and she didn't even have a ticket. Said a group of her friends were in there and that someone else had taken her ticket. She sort of threw a fit—before they threw her out."

Sabrina stopped for a moment. Libby must have meant her—she was the one who had taken the ticket Jun-Ling really should have given to Libby.

"I hear she was screaming and kicking and everything! She is such a freak!"

Sabrina swallowed hard. She didn't know if it felt good or horrible to hear Cee Cee throwing Libby's favorite insult back at her. Libby certainly deserved it. But then, it was a horrible thing to call anyone . . .

She didn't want to think about it. She didn't want to think about anything. Just let Cee Cee's words wash over her and rub out any ideas she'd ever had. "So . . . what else?"

"Oh, there's a *big* story out about Joe White. He says its discrimination to have all girl cheerleaders and he's planning to try out for the squad."

"What a freak! That would totally ruin cheer-leading!" Sabrina said, and she realized in one, horrible flash that she actually cared.

"Yeah! And Jim Dougerty's going to try out with him. He is such a freak . . ." Cee Cee prattled on, dishing and dissing everyone she could think of.

And . . . Sabrina was perfectly happy to let her go on. Being Libby, she was discovering something new: gossiping was fun! She knew she wasn't supposed to feel that way, but she did!

Chapter 8

"Sabrina, Sabrina!" Aunt Hilda said, clicking her tongue. "You should have been more careful." She paced up one side of the living room and down the other, the heels of her sandals making depressions in the carpet.

"I know," Sabrina said. She sat on the couch, her eyes following her aunt. "And every spell has consequences, some of them not so nice, right?"

"Yes, exactly." Aunt Zelda leaned against the door to her study, her arms crossed over her chest, her expression severe. "Sabrina, I think it's about time you learned a lesson."

"And I've got to do all my home chores without magic as a punishment, right?" Sabrina answered.

"You bet!" both aunts chimed in together.

Sabrina smiled and leaned back against the soft pillow, feeling as though she had it made. It was Monday morning and she was going to be late to school. But that didn't matter nearly as much as finding out how to reverse that spell! So Mr. Kraft would make her do detention—so what? It would be better than another one of those killer cheerleader practice sessions this afternoon!

Behind her pacing aunt, the sun poured through the window and birds chirped joyously. Even her neighbor's little white dog had stopped barking for once! They matched Sabrina's own mood. She didn't mind her aunts punishing her because she knew the next thing they were going to do was tell her how to reverse the switcheroo spell. She wouldn't have to be Libby anymore! She wouldn't have to act like Libby or think like her. She wouldn't have to care about cheerleading or feel bored by the newspaper or run around thinking seven-eighths of the people in the world were freaks! It was going to be heavenly!

"Now, I'm sure you've tried to reverse the spell, haven't you?" Aunt Zelda asked.

Sabrina nodded, looking down into her hands, which were folded in her lap. She knew she was in trouble with her aunts so she tried to look serious and remorseful. But inside, she was giggling happily. Her ordeal would be over in just a few minutes. She'd be Sabrina again, not some strange Frankenstein monster who was half Sabrina and half Libby.

"But reversing the spell didn't work, did it?" Aunt Hilda said, still pacing.

Sabrina shook her head. "But I really want it to! So if you'll just tell me the formula, I'll take care of this problem right away and everything will be back to normal." She snapped her fingers, hoping it would be that easy.

But Aunt Zelda was shaking her head and sighing. "I'm afraid it's rather complicated, Sabrina. Switcheroo spells are very serious. You can't reverse them just by saying a spell and pointing."

"You can't?" Sabrina's glee evaporated. Outside, a dark cloud sailed in front of the sun and the birds stopped chirping, suddenly afraid. The dog let out a loud, mournful wail. She picked at a loose thread in the upholstery, nervously tugging at the end until it came free.

Her aunts took a seat, too, one on either side of her. "No. It doesn't work like that," said Aunt Hilda.

"You see, by casting that spell, you wronged Libby," said Aunt Zelda.

"But she's incredibly mean!"

"It doesn't matter. You still wronged her. And by wronging her, you wronged all of Westbridge High, the entire town, in fact, the entire human race!" said Aunt Hilda. Her expression was very serious.

"Oh come on! It can't be that bad!"

"Oh, it is. It is!" said Aunt Zelda.

Sabrina bit her lower lip. She was getting a bad feeling, a very bad feeling. "So . . . what exactly do you mean?"

"What we mean is, no simple little formula can change things back!"

"What?" Sabrina shrieked. She was getting that angry, frustrated feeling she'd come to know so well ever since she and Libby had switched places. What her aunts were saying was, she was stuck! There was no getting out of being Libby! If that was the case, she'd go to the Other Realm and throw herself at the mercy of the Witches' Council. But then, they weren't the most forgiving bunch.

She switched from biting her lips nervously to tearing off chunks of her nails in extreme anxiety. A horrible picture was forming in her head. If she was really stuck as Libby, she'd start thinking more and more like her. Her aunts would start to hate her, just like Val already did. Her grades would slip down as low as Libby's usually were. She wouldn't get into a good college . . . She wouldn't get a good job. She'd be a mean person for the rest of her life. What it meant was that by accidentally casting that dumb switcheroo spell, she'd ruined her whole life.

Sabrina sighed deeply. "Aunt Hilda, Aunt Zelda, I'm so sorry. I've made a terrible mess of things."

"Saying you're sorry won't help," Aunt Zelda insisted. She stroked Sabrina's hair. Her hands were warm. Sabrina wondered how much longer her aunt would feel like comforting her this way. When she was fully Libby, they probably wouldn't even want to be in the same room as her.

Sabrina held back tears. She tried hard to find a bright side. Well, there *was* one thing to be thankful for. Harvey! At least he hadn't switched too and fallen in love with Libby instead of her. Though . . . he hadn't called all weekend. Sabrina bit off the top of a nail with her teeth, thinking how horrible it would be if he were already starting to fall out of love with her.

"Aunt Hilda, Aunt Zelda, I have a question," she said.

"What is it?" Aunt Hilda asked gently.

"Well, Libby and I seem to have traded everything. Lives, friends, even thoughts. But . . . Harvey. He still loves me. At least, I think he does. He didn't suddenly start going out with Libby. Why is that—I mean, Justin Schwartz was in love with Libby but he's switched to me."

Aunt Hilda smiled and clasped her hands together. "Remember, that means it's true love."

"Oh, yeah. I forgot."

"Yes. You see, true love is too honest to switch just because of a spell. It's real, it endures, and even magic can't change it."

"But what about Justin?" Sabrina asked.

Aunt Hilda shrugged. "Must just be a crush. Maybe a very strong crush, but it isn't the real thing. If it were, this boy Justin would still be totally crazy about Libby."

Sabrina considered for a moment. She wished he were. Libby was pretty lonely right now. In this state of mind, she might actually appreciate poor Justin. But they'd never get the chance to know . . .

Sabrina pictured Harvey's smile, his dark hair flopping into his eyes, the feel of his strong arms around her. Yes, Harvey's love was the only bright side in all of this.

"Just do me one favor," Sabrina said, turning toward first one aunt, then to the other and back again.

"What?" they asked together.

"If you ever decide you can't stand me, just remember, we're family so you're stuck with me!"

Aunt Hilda laughed and put her arm around Sabrina's shoulders. "Why would that happen?" she asked.

"Because when I turn totally into Libby, you'll probably hate her as much as I do!" Sabrina shrugged. "And since I'm going to have to be her for the rest of my life, I guess you'll hate me, too."

Aunt Zelda stopped petting Sabrina's hair and looked at her with a confused expression. "And why is it that you think you're going to be Libby for the rest of your life?"

Sabrina caught her breath. A little flame of hope flared in her. "You mean I'm not going to be?"

"Of course not!" her aunts burst out together. Aunt Hilda embraced her and Aunt Zelda messed up her hair fondly with one hand.

"You can't just say a formula and point, but you *can* reverse the spell," Hilda said.

"You have to do one good deed for every twenty-four hours the spell has been in effect," Zelda explained.

"What an amazing relief!" Sabrina gasped. All at once, life was good again. As if to stay in sync with her mood, the cloud slipped away from in front of the sun and the living room brightened.

"Now when, exactly, did you cast this spell?" Aunt Hilda asked.

"Friday morning," Sabrina said. She was overjoyed, ecstatic.

"And today is Monday morning. So . . . one . . . two . . . you have to do three good deeds."

"Piece of cake!" Sabrina crowed. She was feeling more like herself already.

Aunt Zelda shook her head slightly. "Sabrina. It might not be as easy as you expect."

A giggle escaped from deep within Sabrina's

chest. "Why not? I'm a nice person. I do plenty of good deeds, even when I don't have to."

Aunt Hilda sighed, patting Sabrina's hand as if there were something to all this Sabrina didn't understand. "It's true. The Sabrina we know and love could do three good deeds before breakfast and not even realize it."

"Oh, I get it. I'm not allowed to use my magic. That's what makes it hard."

Aunt Zelda *tsk*ed her tongue. "No. Point all you want. A good deed is a good deed, no matter how you accomplish it," she told her.

Sabrina shrugged. "So what's the problem? No, no, no, don't tell me." She held up her hands as if to keep them from saying a word. She didn't want to hear her aunts' bad news. She bounced off the couch, laughing and whirling around, feeling freer than she had in days. "Look, don't worry about me!" she said. "That spell is as good as reversed!" She hurried toward the door and threw it open. She breathed in deeply. Her lungs filling with fresh air and hope.

"Sabrina! Wait!" Aunt Hilda called after her.

But the door slammed shut behind her. She was already gone.

Sabrina stood on the corner of Pine Street and Ridge Avenue, waiting. Across the street was the mall, gleaming huge and boxy in the sun. Cars whizzed by. People strolled along looking in shop windows or hurried past on their way to someplace important. A few kids skateboarded past. A couple went by on a bicycle built for two. A spring breeze rustled the leaves of the oak trees that spanned the street on either side. What was she waiting for? She wasn't sure. But if she stood around long enough, a good deed was bound to show up.

Ah, there one was. A woman was crossing the street. Her white hair was pinned into a messy bun and she stood very bent over as she walked, using her cane. She was struggling under the weight of a heavy bag of groceries, which she carried with one arm. A carton of eggs poked out of the top, right next to a big bag of juicy tomatoes. Her thick glasses kept slipping off her nose and each time she reached one finger up to push them back up, the bag would sink a little lower onto her hip.

"Hey lady! Lady!" Sabrina called waving at her. The woman looked up and the bag slipped just a fraction of an inch lower. Sabrina had a vague feeling she wasn't doing this exactly right but she didn't care. Aunt Zelda had said a good deed was a good deed, no matter how you accomplished it.

She skipped over to the woman. "Hey, that looks heavy," she said.

"It is," the woman answered.

"Maybe you can get someone to help you with it," Sabrina countered.

The woman shot her a dirty look. *Ooops,* Sabrina thought. That was Libby talking. "What I meant was, maybe *I* can help you with it." She reached her arms out to take the bag. The woman smiled and held it out toward her.

But before she could take it out of the woman's grasp and into her own, a voice called her from behind. "Sabrina! Hey, Sabrina!" She turned to find Cee Cee and Jill waving at her from the mall parking lot. They both had their hair pulled into pigtails.

"Hi!" Sabrina waved.

"We're going to the record store. Screaming Broccoli's signing CDs over there! Come on!"

"Oh wow!" Sabrina said excitedly. "Just hold on a second, I've got to—" she started to turn back to the old woman . . .

Keeerashhhhh. Sabrina heard the horrible sound with a sinking feeling in the pit of her stomach.

"Oh no, oh no, oh no!" The old woman was moaning, bending over the fallen bag of groceries. A head of lettuce rolled under a car along with a few cans of prunes. The tomatoes had tumbled all over the street and lay in a smushed, bright red mess. The carton of eggs lay upside-down in the gutter.

Oh no, oh no, oh no! Sabrina moaned right along with her. She'd missed a golden opportunity to perform her first good deed. How could it have happened—how? The real Sabrina would never have stopped to say hello to anyone until that bag had been safely in her arms. But she already knew that she wasn't exactly the same old Sabrina. Sometimes she was. At other times, bits of Libby just took over.

"Please, help me get those cans," the woman said to Sabrina, pointing to a few that had rolled into the street, "before someone drives along and runs over them," she said.

Oh good. This could be her good deed. It wasn't a big one, but maybe that wouldn't matter. She started to go after the cans. But it was too late. The light had turned from red to green and the traffic was already on its way. *Whoozh*, the cars went. Sabrina took a step back up onto the curb. *Smuuush*, went the cans.

Oh no! I should have used my magic to make that light stay red a few moments longer, Sabrina thought. She turned away, feeling certain there was nothing more she could do. At the same moment, the woman reached toward the carton of eggs and turned it right-side up. She started to lift up the top.

"Wait!" Sabrina cried. She began to point.

But it was too late. The woman had already opened the carton. "Broken! Every single one!" she moaned, staring at the gooey yellow mush that ran through the egg cups.

Missed another chance! Sabrina chastised herself. She could have used her magic to make those eggs whole again before the woman saw they were broken. It wouldn't have been a big thing, just a little one to make this poor woman's day a little better. And maybe it would have been enough to count as a good deed, who knew?

She turned away, heading toward Cee Cee and Jill, too embarrassed even to say she was sorry to the woman. She heard a man's voice speaking to the woman. "Let me help you pick those things up, ma'am," he said politely.

"Thank you *so* much," the woman answered. "You know, when you're fragile, like I am, every little bit of help really counts."

Sabrina slapped her forehead. *Darn!* The real Sabrina would have had those groceries picked up in a heartbeat. What's more, she would have been able to think of a dozen other nice things to do for this woman . . . and she hadn't even been able to do one!

Chapter 9

"Omigosh! It's Joe Crooner!" Cee Cee squealed. She pointed at the lean, muscular singer, his head bent over a blue-haired fan's CD, his hand scrawling yet another signature.

"This is soooo great!" Jill sighed. She pushed against the person in line in front of her as if that would get them to the head of the line an instant or two sooner.

"Do you think we'll get to talk to them? I really want to ask Joe Crooner how he comes up with all those incredible lyrics!"

"If we get up to the front at all! The guy at the door said the band's on a tight schedule and they may not get to sign everybody's stuff."

"We've just *got* to see them. I'll *die* if we don't."

Sabrina had to admit, she'd be pretty disappointed herself. She'd seen Screaming Broccoli in concert, but it was different actually meeting the band up close, even if it was only for a few moments. At least they were pretty near the front of the line, so at least there was a good possibility they'd get to the front. Those saps at the back didn't have a chance! She jiggled her leg impatiently. If only she could point and make all these people disappear! Then it would be just her and Cee Cee and Jill with Joe and Luke, Dingbat and Maureen. Come to think of it, she'd make Cee Cee and Jill disappear, too. Why share?

Sabrina sighed as she realized the Libby-ish thoughts that had gone through her mind. How was she ever going to get any good deeds done with that kind of thinking? She'd failed so miserably with the old woman crossing the street. It had really scared her.

She looked around the room, searching for a good deed waiting to be done. The line of fans flared out, with everyone talking excitedly and pushing slightly. Some of them were wearing khaki pants and button-down shirts tucked in. Others were in ripped T-shirts and black boots. Yet others were decked out in tie-dyed pants and beads. Screaming Broccoli had a diverse following. No matter what their style, the fans feasted their eyes on the band, sitting behind a big table at the front of the store. Sabrina recognized Alison Watanabe at the head of the line, her dark hair pulled back into a neat ponytail, her black T-shirt proudly proclaiming "I love Joe!"

"I had the *best time* at the concert the other night!" Sabrina heard Alison exclaim.

"Glad you enjoyed it. We loved playing, too," Joe Crooner said mechanically, as if he'd said it a thousand times before. Sabrina watched as he scribbled his name on Alison's CD without even glancing at her.

It sure would be nice if he looked up at her and smiled, she thought.

She could use her magic powers to make that happen. It would be such a small thing, but so nice. Maybe when it was her own turn, she'd do just that. Vaguely, she had a sense that she was missing something, but she wasn't sure exactly what. She saw Alison heave a small, disappointed sigh, then move on to Luke Lowlife. She pushed her CD under the guitarist's pen, but he didn't look at her either.

Libby moved into the place Alison had just left. "I love you guys. You're the best!" she said.

"Thanks." Joe Crooner signed her CD without even a flicker of his eyes in her direction. He let out a long, loud yawn. He looked so bored he was almost asleep at the table.

As Cee Cee and Jill chattered excitedly beside her, Sabrina tried to understand why the band would act that way. In the interviews she'd read, they didn't seem like they took their fans for granted. They did their fair share of community work, raising money through free concerts for everything from homeless families to rain forest preservation. They seemed like caring people. But the endless publicity must get incredibly tiring. Imagine going out to pick up a quart of milk at the supermarket and being mobbed by fans. Or having to sign CDs at twenty-five cities across the United States in twenty-five days. No wonder they went on automatic!

Sabrina licked her lips, studying the band. There was Luke, wiping beads of sweat from his handsome forehead. Dingbat was stuffing a piece of gum in his mouth and chewing sloppily. Maureen was tapping out a bored rhythm on the table with her fingers while she waited for the next CD to be shoved under her nose.

Suddenly Sabrina knew. That would be her first good deed! All she had to do was point and she could solve all the problems Joe and Luke and Dingbat and Maureen faced every day. She could make it so that no one recognized them until they stepped on a stage or in front of a publicity camera. Or she could cast a spell so that every single fan was sensitive and careful to respect their privacy. Or she could change the band themselves so that they actually enjoyed all the publicity around them. There were so many things she could do!

Sabrina was jostled out of her thoughts by the pushing of the crowd. People were starting to get impatient. "They've got to leave by twelve-thirty to get to their next gig!" she heard a boy with a pierced eyebrow saying behind her. "After that, the store's going to throw all of us out, whether we've gotten our CDs signed or not!"

Sabrina checked her watch. "It's already 12:23," she told Cee Cee and Jill, staring at the orange numbers of the watch. She counted the number of people in front of them. "Twenty-one . . . twenty-two . . . twenty-three . . . bad news, guys—there's no way we'll ever make it!"

"This is so unfair!" Cee Cee complained.

"Yeah! All those freaks got their CDs signed and we're not going to even see the band!" Jill agreed.

Disappointment twisted through Sabrina's throat. Cee Cee and Jill were right. It wasn't fair. They'd waited just like everyone else! She scanned the crowd. People were frowning, shoving, crying. One boy had ducked down and was crawling through people's feet, trying to get through to the front. A girl tripped over him and fell with a loud *klunk*. "Oww. My knee!" Sabrina heard her cry. But the crowd kept pushing and two more people fell over the downed girl.

"*Mmf.*"

"*Uggh,*" they moaned.

The store staff was trying to defuse the situation but from what Sabrina could see, they were only making things worse. "All right, people, let's move on out of here," one of them called out. The crowd responded with boos, hisses, and jeers. As the staff tried to direct fans toward the exits, people began pushing their way toward the band, who were still quietly signing the last few CDs as if nothing at all were happening. As the crowd pushed forward, people tripped over the downed kids and fell themselves. "Ouch!" someone said. "I hurt my ankle!"

This is a truly dangerous situation, Sabrina thought. She'd heard about people getting trampled at concerts and stuff. She couldn't believe how out of hand the situation had gotten so quickly.

And she could save it! All she had to do was point and everyone would find themselves magically transported outside, away from danger. Or she could use magic to put the kids on the floor back on their feet. No one would fall over them and get hurt. Or she could cast a spell to delay Screaming Broccoli's flight. Then they'd be able to sign a few more CDs and everyone would be happy. What was more, whatever she chose to do, it would count as her first good deed and she'd be that much closer to being herself again. So which good deed should she do . . .

At that moment, however, there was a squawking over the public address system and the manager's voice blared out, "I'm sorry, people, but Screaming Broccoli are going to have to leave now. They'll be signing just one more CD. So let's be reasonable, folks, and let's all get out of here without anybody getting hurt!"

In that moment, Sabrina panicked, along with half the others in the crowd.

"I've got to see them!"

"Get out of my way. I'm going to be that last fan whose CD they sign!"

"Yoww, you're hurting me."

"Move it, freak!"

Sabrina pointed. But instead of the crowd moving outside, instead of the fallen fans being on their feet, instead of there being a last-minute notification about a late flight, what happened was that Sabrina found herself popped to the front of the line. "Great!" she exclaimed, pumping her fist in the air. "I'm first on line! Hey, Joe Crooner, sign my CD!" Behind her, she could hear people yelling.

"All right, all right!" she heard someone saying. It was a police officer and he and his buddies were already herding people out of the store. The situation cooled off immediately. People grumbled, but they stopped pushing—no thanks to Sabrina and her magic, though.

Oh no! Another good deed missed! she thought. Of course, it was good no one was going to leave the store with anything more than a bruised knee. But what about her? She was still Libby!

She didn't worry about it too long, however, because a pimply faced staff member was motioning her forward. She was just taking the first step when she noticed a girl sobbing behind her. She looked as though she was about thirteen. Tears poured down her round, plain face. "I am soooo upset," she moaned. "I came all the way from Boston to see the Broccoli. I convinced my mom to take the afternoon off from work to do it. And now I'm not going to see them! And after I missed the concert Friday night because the stupid car broke down! I actually had the tickets in my hand and I couldn't use them!" she wailed.

Sabrina looked at the girl's unhappy face, thinking how stupid it was to be that upset! Even if she did get a chance to get her CD signed, none of the band members would even look at her. This girl must be totally a loser and a freak! She began to walk toward Joe Crooner, who was picking his teeth with a toothpick and looking with longing toward the window and the world beyond it.

In the next instant, Sabrina stopped herself. Wait a minute. So what if the girl was a little pathetic? She'd be so incredibly happy if she could get her dumb CD signed. When Sabrina thought about it, it wasn't the girl who was a loser, it was Sabrina herself. Had she really used her powers to put herself at the front of the line? Wasn't that cheating? And the only thought she'd given to the pushing and the crowd had been whether they'd mess up her chance to meet the band! She'd been selfish, selfish, totally selfish!

"Come on!" the staff guy with the acne said to Sabrina. "So you want your CD signed or not?"

She looked at the girl again, then down at the CD in her hand. Yeah, why not go ahead and do it? Sabrina had actually heard the Broccoli, which was the important thing, while this girl had missed the concert. Having Joe Crooner ignore her while he signed her CD meant almost nothing to her, while it would mean the world to this kid.

Sabrina turned and caught the girl's teary eyes. "Hey you!" she said. "Why don't you go ahead of me?"

The girl's eyes widened as if she'd just seen her guardian angel. "Do you really mean it?" She started to cry all over again, but this time joyfully. "But if I do that, you won't get your own CD signed."

Sabrina nibbled on a fingernail. It really would be fun to have a signed CD . . .

The pimply faced staff person stepped in again. "Come on, now. Let's get this over with. One of you step up. After that, we're closing this circus down!"

Sabrina looked at the girl's hopeful face and

shrugged. She motioned the girl forward. "Go ahead," she said. "I think this will mean a little more to you than it does to me."

The girl's face lit up with an expression of bliss. "Oooo, thank you!" she breathed, looking thrilled. She stepped toward Joe Crooner and laid her CD on the table. He pulled it toward him, his eyes focused intently on the table. That's when Sabrina pointed. Joe Crooner lifted up his eyes to meet the girl's. He held them for one intense moment. And then . . . then, very slowly, he smiled!

"Uhh!" the girl groaned ecstatically. In the next instant, she fainted. While the staff people ran to get water or fanned her with their hands, Sabrina grinned. One good deed down, two more to go!

sky over Westbridge red and orange, and she'd accomplished only one good deed—making that girl's day at the CD signing! It was so awful. She'd thought completing three good deeds would be as easy as eating a piece of chocolate cake. But she hadn't counted on the Libby factor. She just wasn't thinking the way she usually did.

Crummy day, she thought. The only thing she could think of to make herself feel better was to call Harvey. But then, she was mad at him, too. He hadn't called all weekend. When she'd finally talked to him, he'd made up some big excuse, saying the team had been exhausted after the games and, finally, too depressed by their defeat at the last moment by the Ridgefield team to talk to anyone. True, he'd phoned the moment he'd gotten home . . . but Sabrina thought he ought to pay a little more attention. Or maybe it was Libby who thought that. By now, it was too hard to figure out whose thoughts were whose!

She marched down the street toward home, too engrossed in her thoughts to greet Mrs. Wintergreen or stop to say hello to the Knickerbocker kids. She stared at the gray concrete, with her square-toed flats kicking across it. What could she do, what could she do? She wracked her brain for possible good deeds. She could give Mr. Kraft a very bad flu. All the kids at school would think that was a very good thing indeed. Probably, even the Witches' Council would count it. But Mr. Kraft definitely wouldn't . . . Sabrina considered it. It wasn't really fair to do something that was a good deed for some people but a bad one to somebody else. *I better be careful,* she thought. *I don't want to waste any good deeds.*

As the words formed in her head, she stopped in her tracks. *What am I thinking?* she chastised herself. *There's no such thing as wasting a good deed. The more the better!*

Suddenly, she felt desperate. It was like living with a ghost inside her—Libby's ghost! The old Sabrina wouldn't have taken all day to do one little good deed. She would have done a dozen by now!

She stared around wildly, frantic to do a good deed right there, that moment, and prove to herself that she was still more Sabrina than Libby. The spring flowers in Mrs. Wintergreen's garden were drooping. She could water them or simply point and up they'd perk. She could make the boo-boo on the Knickerbocker kid's knee heal up. She could fill the gas tank of someone whose dashboard said empty. She could . . .

But what was that horrible noise distracting her thoughts. *Roooff. Roooff. Roooff.* A dog was barking. *That stupid Del Vecchio dog,* Sabrina thought. *Dumb mutt. Just a mop of dirty white hair. And always barking!*

Hmmm. Maybe there was a good deed to be done right there! She could shut the dog up. All the neighbors would appreciate that. Or better yet, point the annoying creature into outer space. But then, the Del Vecchio kid would be devastated. Heart broken. Teary-eyed. No, that wasn't a very good deed, not at all, once she began thinking about it.

She sat down on the curb, watching the dog. It was tied by a very short rope to a concrete patio. It kept running and leaping, trying to get free, but the rope kept jerking it back. Just beyond its reach was a soft, fresh green lawn, with yummy smelling flowers, squirrels just begging to be chased, and a dusty patch perfect for digging up and burying things in. No wonder the dog barked so much. It was like putting a candy bar in front of a kid and telling her she couldn't eat it!

Sabrina smiled to herself, knowing what her next good deed would be. She pointed and the rope that tied the dog lengthened. The dog ran, leaped . . . and sailed forward onto the lawn. *Arrroooooo!* it howled gleefully. It took off, zipping around the grass, sniffing everything, chasing a bumblebee. And, no big surprise, it stopped it's constant *roof*fing.

Great! Two good deeds done. Just one more left!

Three days later, Sabrina found herself finishing up her third good deed. She'd gone over to the Ridgefield food pantry and helped feed some of the hungry people of the area. All afternoon, she'd packed bags of groceries with cans of beans and cartons of spaghetti, packets of lunch meats, oranges, a bunch of asparagus . . . Then, as the people had come in, she'd helped hand out the bags. Some of them had been ragged, with old, torn clothes and dirt under their fingernails. Others had dressed just like anyone else. They could have been a neighbor, a friend's mother, a grandparent—and they probably were! But Sabrina had noticed an embarrassed, exhausted look in their eyes. It was incredible how many people needed help. You never would have known it to look at the clean, well-kept streets, homes and stores in and around Ridgefield.

Sabrina lifted one of the last bags into the arms of a strong, athletic red-haired boy. He was wearing a Ridgefield baseball jacket and Sabrina recognized him as one of the star batters of Westbridge's rival team. She gave him a quick smile but she didn't say anything to let on that she knew who he was. She didn't want to make him feel embarrassed.

Now that she'd done it, Sabrina realized that working at the food pantry was one of the best things she'd ever done. She'd meant to go days ago but she'd always felt too beat after cheerleading practice or there'd been something on TV she wanted to see or Harvey had invited her out to get a burger. Sure, she'd come out of self-interest this time—she needed to reverse that spell. But next time, she'd come just because she wanted to. That would be an even better good deed.

When all the bags were all gone, Sabrina went over to Kathleen, the woman who ran the pantry, to say good-bye. "Thanks so much for helping!" Kathleen said. She gave Sabrina a big hug. "Come on back any time—we really appreciate the help!"

"Thanks to you, too. I'll definitely be back. It was fun!" Sabrina said, and she meant it. She felt as though the Libby inside her had receded just a little with each minute she'd spent at the food pantry. She waved and stepped outside.

The sky was bright and the sun, starting to dip in the sky, felt warm against her skin. Now what? She'd done her three good deeds. Now how would the spell reverse itself? Would it just happen? Or did she have to perform some ritual first? She closed her eyes and tried to see if she could feel Libby inside her. Did she feel like her old self? She thought she did. She couldn't tell for sure.

Oh, of course you're yourself! she told herself. *You did your three good deeds. The spell is broken!*

Sabrina walked out back behind the food pantry building to the parking lot. Rays of sun glinted off the metal hoods of the cars. Sabrina found hers—or, rather, her aunts'; they'd lent it to her when she'd told them where she was going—and got in. She revved the engine and put it in gear, then stepped on the gas and headed over to the Slicery. Harvey had told her to meet him there after she was done. Maybe Val and Gordie would be there, too. She could see her friends. Celebrate getting back to herself again!

Fifteen minutes later, she was pushing open the Slicery door. The smell of tomatoes, cheese, and grease wafted out of the kitchen. Someone had cued up Screaming Broccoli's newest hit, *Getting Back to the Girl I Used to Be.* Sabrina's eyes surveyed the noisy tables. At a booth in the corner, Harvey was relaxing with a few of his buddies from the baseball team. One lone crust of pizza lay in the silver tray. Dirty white paper plates were scattered across the table. The guys chewed the last of their slices or downed long swigs of soda. Sabrina sauntered over, feeling on the top of the world.

"Hey, Sabrina!" Harvey said. He gave her a big kiss as the guys squashed over in the booth and she squeezed in next to him.

"Hi everyone!" she said, feeling happy.

"So . . . what do you want?" Harvey asked her.

Sabrina didn't have to look at a menu. "I'll have a pineapple and pepperoni slice. And a diet coke."

"Okay then! Here comes Justin to take your

order." Harvey pointed at the waiter, who was on his way over.

Justin kicked toward the table, shrugging shyly. "Hi, Sabrina," he said, not looking in her eyes.

"Hi Justin." She felt embarrassed talking to him too, after their silly movie date. She peeked over at Harvey. Was there a little jealous look in his eyes? She'd told him she'd gone to the movies with Justin—just as a friendly thing . . . but maybe someone had told him they'd held hands . . . Thank goodness all that was over! Now that she and Libby were safely themselves again, things could go back to the way they used to be—and Justin would never give her a second look.

Justin stood there, his pen poised over his order book. "I'm . . . really glad to see you," he said, daring to meet Sabrina's eyes. She stared at him. Uh-oh. Was that a lovesick expression on his face? Was he still mooning over her like a puppy dog? No. *No!* Could it be that Justin still had his crush on her? Could she and Libby still be switched? She looked around the Slicery. Everyone chatted happily, eating and laughing. The scene certainly *looked* normal. But she was getting a terrible feeling that all was still not right.

And then she realized what she'd just said to Harvey. *"I'll have a pineapple and pepperoni slice. And a diet coke."* The real Sabrina wouldn't have ordered that if she'd been shipwrecked and hadn't seen the inside of a kitchen for ten years!

"Auuurgh," Sabrina cried, balling her hands into little fists.

Darn it! She'd done her good deeds, but she was still Libby! It wasn't fair! Something had gone horribly wrong.

Chapter 11

"It's not fair! Your stupid reversaroo spell didn't work!" Sabrina yelled at her aunts.

She clattered the dishes on purpose as she twirled them around in the soapy water. If she was going to have to do her house chores by hand, at least it should be a little annoying to her aunts, too. It was so dumb—all she had to do was point and this entire mess would go away.

She was angry, that was for sure, but not about the dishes. It was the fact that her aunts' solution to the switcheroo spell had been about as effective as a broken remote control. More than angry, she was scared! What if she had to stay Libby forever? She groaned miserably, rinsing a plate and slamming it none-too-gently into the plastic dish rack. She reached into the soapy water and pulled out another, letting the water spray over it furiously.

"Please. Calm down!" Aunt Hilda said. She laid a hand on Sabrina's shoulder. "Getting upset isn't going to help . . ."

"And neither is breaking the china!" Aunt Zelda added. She removed the plate from Sabrina's hand and placed it gently in the dish rack. Then she ushered her into one of the kitchen chairs. "Sit down and try to cool off just a little."

"And talk to us instead of yelling!" Aunt Hilda insisted.

Sabrina sighed, shaking her head. "I'm sorry." She shook the water off her hands and, pointing, conjured up a dish towel to wipe them on. "I didn't mean to shout. It's just that . . . I did the three good deeds you told me about and . . . what good did it do me? None! I'm still Libby, Libby's still me, and I'm about as close to a solution as I was the first day this stupid spell got cast."

"Hold on, hold on!" Aunt Hilda said. She plunked herself into the chair next to Sabrina's and cupped her niece's chin with her hand. "Number one, you don't do a good deed for yourself, you do it for someone else."

Sabrina slid her chin away. "I know, I know. And that's just the point! See, the real Sabrina never would have said something like that. That's Libby talking! And she's not supposed to be here anymore, not after all those good deeds."

Aunt Zelda shook her head. "That isn't the way it works."

Sabrina cocked her head quizzically. "What do you mean? You said one good deed for every day I was Libby. And I was Libby for Friday, Saturday, and Sunday . . . three days so three good deeds."

Aunt Zelda licked her lips. "Uh, I hate to break the bad news to you, Sabrina, but . . . how many days did it take you to accomplish your good deeds?"

Sabrina frowned. "Well, let's see, it's Wednesday now so . . . three days."

Aunt Hilda took her hand and squeezed it. "Math isn't my strong point but . . . doesn't the three days from Friday to Sunday plus the three days from Monday to Wednesday make . . . six days?"

Aunt Zelda nodded. "Six days, six good deeds. You're still three short, sweetheart."

"Wha???" Sabrina gasped as the truth hit her.

"That's right. While you were busy making good things happen, more time passed . . . and with this spell, that means more good deeds," Aunt Hilda explained.

"So I suggest you move a little more quickly," Aunt Zelda said, "to get the rest of your good things done or . . ."

"Or I'll stay Libby forever!" Sabrina wailed.

"That's right!" her aunts said together.

Sabrina sunk her forehead into her hand. As her real self, it would have been possible. But as Libby there was just no way she could do it. There were too many distractions and interruptions, too many friends to see, too much fun to have. "I'm doomed," she said.

"Sabrina! You're not doomed!" Aunt Zelda insisted.

"It's not that hard to do three good deeds," Aunt Hilda agreed.

Sabrina got up, feeling far too anxious to sit still. "No, but it's hard to do them fast enough so that you don't need to do more. Especially when you're stuck being Libby!" She began pacing up one length of the kitchen and down the next, kicking angrily at the floor.

"Oh come on, Sabrina. It isn't that hard. Use your imagination!" Aunt Zelda insisted.

"Libby doesn't have one, at least not when it comes to being nice!"

"But you're not Libby! You're Sabrina!" Aunt Hilda pointed out.

Sabrina made yet another turn up the kitchen. "Yeah, but that part of me is buried so deep, I barely even know she's there!"

Aunt Zelda frowned. "Well then I suggest you stop complaining and dig for her." There wasn't even a teaspoon of sympathy in her tone.

Aunt Hilda was a little more gentle. "You need to get in touch with your inner Sabrina," she said.

Sabrina sighed. Her inner Sabrina. Was she even still there anymore? She seemed to grow smaller and smaller all the time, like an ice cube in the sun. "How do I do that?" she wailed.

Aunt Hilda wrapped her arm around her. "It's not nearly as hard as you think, honey. Just try doing some of the things you used to do and spend time with the people who used to be your friends."

She could sort of see Aunt Hilda's point. What she was saying was that Sabrina had lost touch with herself because she hadn't been doing the things she normally would do. She was beginning to think like Libby because she was being forced by circumstances to act like her.

But as for Aunt Hilda's solution—it just seemed impossible. How could she see her old friends if they hated her and how could she do her old activities if not with those friends? On the other hand, what else could she do—give up? No, because then she'd have to live with being Libby forever. And that was one alternative that she just couldn't accept.

What would the real Sabrina do if she were in a situation like this one? Sabrina asked herself, trying to think like her old self. Then the answer came to her. *She'd believe in her friends! She'd trust them. And she'd get help from them.* That was it! They might not know it right now, but they cared about her! Somewhere, deep down, they liked and cared about her, despite the switcheroo.

A plan was forming in her head. Maybe, just maybe, if she got everyone together—all the people who made up her life before the change and after it—things would sort themselves out in her head. She'd be able to do just what Aunt Hilda had said—get in touch with her "inner Sabrina."

Sure, that was it! She had a feeling the real Sabrina would just slip back into place once she saw all of them lined up together—Harvey and Val and Gordie and . . . and hey, even Cee Cee and Jill and . . . and most of all, Libby! And once the real Sabrina was back in her brain, those good deeds would be easier than popping popcorn. In fact, the more she thought about it, the more sure of it she was.

"Thanks Aunt Hilda, Aunt Zelda! Thanks a million!"

"What'd we do?" Aunt Hilda asked Aunt Zelda.

"Shhh. Don't ask. Just take the credit," Aunt Zelda whispered.

Sabrina barely listened. She was sure this was going to work out perfectly. Now, she just had to bite the bullet and stay Libby for one more day. Tomorrow, after school, she was going to make everything okay once and for all!

Chapter 12

"I need that computer! I'm late with this story! Get off that keyboard now!" Joe Lasko said.

"You can't have it. *I'm* late with *my* story!" Val responded.

Sabrina stood in the doorway of the *Lantern* office, itching at Libby's cheerleader uniform, taking in the scene. The sound of a printer churning out copy drummed through the room, someone was chattering on the phone and a small portable radio leaked a tinny version of the latest Screaming Broccoli hit into the room. Articles were strewn on top of any desk they happened to land on, wastebaskets overflowed, a few candy bar wrappers and empty soda cans lay on the top of a scratched file cabinet. Ms. Quick split her attention among three students, all demanding an answer to an urgent question that very second.

This used to be where I hung out, Sabrina thought. The week since she'd been in here felt like forever. But what else did she feel? Did she miss it? Or was she glad to leave the mess and chaos behind? She closed her eyes, took a deep breath, and looked deep into her heart. She was pleased to realize that she felt a little sorry not to have been around here for a while. *Good!* she thought. *That's a little piece of the real Sabrina that's still left in me!* She focused on the feeling so that she could remember it and summon it up when she needed it.

"So . . . Sabrina Spellman. What are *you* doing here?"

Sabrina opened her eyes to find Val's dark gaze staring her down. She ran her fingers through her hair, suddenly wanting to make a good impression. "Remember when I called you I . . . uh . . . I told you I wanted to write a story?" she improvised. In fact, she hadn't really thought about what she'd say to Val when she actually saw her. But she knew she needed to get her old friend in on the meeting. She'd never get in touch with her inner Sabrina without her.

Val made a face. "Yeah, but I didn't think you were serious!"

"I am! And what I want to write about is . . . is

this food pantry over in Ridgefield. I volunteered there the other day."

"You did?!" Val seemed shocked.

"Yeah, I did!" Sabrina answered, annoyed at how surprised Val looked. Then again, what did it matter. Sure, Val didn't respect her—but only because she thought she had Libby's personality. The important thing wasn't the story, or even the food pantry. It was getting her and Libby sorted out once and for all!

"Look, I've got to talk to you about it a little more before I start writing the article . . ." Sabrina ad-libbed.

"I've got a little time to talk right now," Val countered. She crossed her arms over her chest as if she'd never believe Sabrina would really write an article until she actually had the copy in her hands. *Hey, the real Sabrina popped out articles every week!* Sabrina felt like reminding her. She suddenly missed her old self. She liked the way she used to be!

"I . . . I can't talk right now." Val rolled her eyes as if she'd expected Sabrina to say something like that. "But can you meet me in, oh . . ." she looked at her watch, "about half an hour at the football field?"

Val groaned. "What could meeting you in the football field possibly have to do with a story about a food pantry?"

Sabrina bit her lower lip. Val was going to say

no. She could feel it. What should she do? Cast a mind control spell? Just pop her out onto the field against her will? She stared into Val's eyes, willing her former friend to remember somewhere in the back of her mind all the lunches they'd shared, every name they'd made up about Mr. Kraft, each party they'd crashed together. But she knew it wouldn't work. Val thought she was Libby. They'd never get past that.

Then Val opened her mouth and said something Sabrina never thought she'd hear in a million years. She said okay.

"Gordie, how important is that science experiment?" Sabrina crashed into the science lab, interrupting Gordie as he was about to pour one beaker of steaming liquid into another. He was wearing goggles to protect his eyes. His hair was about a half an inch long and stood on end—the result of one of those lousy haircuts he kept getting because of Val's newspaper story.

"It's very important!" he answered. "For instance, if I don't get these two compounds mixed immediately, then . . ."

Sabrina had visions of the entire school blowing up. "Then what?"

"Then there won't be any Jell-O for the school lunch tomorrow. That's what I'm making," he said, focusing hard as he continued to pour.

Sabrina laughed. "Look, Gordie, put that away!"

"But the Jell-O!"

Sabrina scowled. "It doesn't matter. The school lunch will stink no matter what you do to it. Besides, I'm . . . I'm doing a kind of chemistry experiment myself. Out on the football field. And I desperately need your help."

It wasn't exactly a lie. She *was* doing a chemistry experiment. Get all those people together and see what the chemistry was. Figure out if they could transform the person she'd become back into the person she used to be.

Gordie studied Sabrina. "This is some kind of trick, isn't it? You're just joking, aren't you?"

Sabrina sighed. "I've never been more serious in my life." She was worried. There was no reason for Gordie to trust her. "Look," she appealed to him. "All you have to do is meet me at the football field in . . ." she checked her watch again, "twenty minutes. It'll be easy."

"But why would I do that? You aren't very nice to me, you know. We aren't friends, never have been."

Sabrina thought. He was right. Even when she'd been Sabrina, Gordie hadn't exactly been a pal. Once he'd started going out with Val, they'd spent a certain amount of time together, but that was different. Still, she somehow knew it was very, very important for Gordie to be at the gathering. "Do it because . . . because if you don't, I'll call you a freak for the rest of the year!"

Gordie put his beaker down firmly on the lab table. "But you'll do that anyway!"

Sabrina shrugged. It was true. Or at least, it would be true if she stayed Libby. No, she didn't want that to be her future. "Come!" she said. Then she looked at him beseechingly and said, "please?"

Gordie studied her face long and hard. Would he say he'd do it or would he ditch out?

"Okay!" Gordie said.

"Woohoo!" Sabrina said, pumping her fist in victory. Then she dashed out of the science lab, seeking others.

"Cee Cee, Jill, where are you guys going?" Sabrina caught them as they were getting into Cee Cee's little red convertible.

"If you really want to know, we were going shopping. There's a big sale on at Skirts and Things." Then Cee Cee put her hand to her mouth as if she'd let out a huge secret. "Oooh. I really didn't mean to tell you that!"

"Yeah. A head cheerleader who misses practice shouldn't get the lowdown on the best sales!" chastised Jill.

Sabrina nibbled her lower lip guiltily. She felt really bad. After going to a few practices, she wasn't nearly as sore as she had been the first day. Besides, she had a responsibility to the team . . . but gathering all her friends and cleaning up the mess of her identity had just seemed a whole lot more important.

"I'm sorry. I really am," she said. "I promise I won't miss practice again." And she wouldn't. Because soon, she wouldn't be Libby anymore and no one would expect to see her at cheerleading.

"Huh!" Cee Cee said, as if she'd believe it when she saw it.

Sabrina took a deep breath. It was going to be a hard thing to say to Cee Cee and Jill, but she had to say it. "I . . . I really need your help. I'm . . . having a little trouble. Actually, big trouble," she said, sighing at last. "I hope you aren't too mad at me," she added. "I really need you."

Cee Cee snorted. "Mad? Oh, we're not mad!" She glanced at Jill as if to say, "Boy, are we ever!"

Jill returned the look, then peeked over at Sabrina. "Well, what do you want?"

"I'll . . . I'll tell you . . . if you meet me at the football field in—" she checked her watch, "fifteen minutes."

Cee Cee and Jill smiled, but there was something not so nice in their expression. "Oh, we'll be there."

"You can count on us!" Jill seconded.

"Great!" Sabrina said. She was a little surprised they'd been so agreeable. But then, they *were* Libby's best friends. And that's what best friends were for. "See you there!" she said. She turned and ran off. Now, all she needed to do was get the last two people she needed for her meeting. Once everyone was there, it would be a snap to channel her old self back into her brain.

"See you!" Cee Cee said.

Sabrina wasn't sure, but as she ran across the front lawn of the school toward the track field, she thought she heard an engine start up and a car drive off.

"Way to go, Harvey!"

"Great time!"

Sabrina caught up with her boyfriend just as he was coming off a timed sprint. His teammates continued to circle the track while he bent over panting. The baseball season had ended in total disgrace, with the Westbridge Scallions missing an easy out and allowing the Ridgefield team to take the statewide championships. But there was Harvey, the very next week, out with the track team, sweating, burning nonexistent fat and training to win.

"Harvey!" Sabrina called to him, running up and giving his sweaty body a huge hug.

"Hi!" Harvey said, nuzzling her hair. "What's up?"

Sabrina brushed her lips lightly over his. At least this was one person she knew would show up for her no matter what. "I need you," she said huskily. "Can you meet me at the football field in ten minutes?"

"Of course!" Harvey said. "Just give me a chance to change out of these sweaty workout clothes."

"See you there!" Sabrina said. She gave him one last kiss, then ran off. There was only one more person to invite to the meeting now. The most important person of all. Libby!

Libby was already halfway home by the time Sabrina caught up with her. She was kicking her shoes against the ground, not looking particularly happy. Her designer bag was slung over one shoulder and she was staring at her feet. "Libby! Hey, Libby!" Sabrina called, trying to catch her breath as she ran up to her.

Libby turned. "Oh, it's you," she said. She didn't sound as angry as she had the last few times Sabrina had talked to her. More resigned.

"How . . . how are you doing?" Sabrina asked. For the first time, she felt kind of bad for Libby. Mean as she was to everyone, it must be pretty confusing to have your whole life switch around under your nose without even realizing why.

"I'm okay," Libby answered. "Life's been a little surreal lately, but I'm getting used to it. I keep getting these strange urges to be nice to people! Do good deeds. Things like that. And you know what? I'm actually finding that I enjoy it! It's so weird!"

"Yeah, isn't it?" Sabrina said, thinking about how she'd actually begin to like cheerleading practice.

She remembered how she'd said she'd never, ever join forces with Libby. But now, she was beginning to see that maybe she could. Not only could, but had to! There was really no way out of this situation unless she could get in touch with her old self and get those good deeds done fast. Besides, Libby wasn't really all that bad. At least, not the Libby that Libby had become over the past few days.

"Of course, there are the *really* obnoxious urges," Libby was saying. "Like when something inside me has this strange desire to sit down at Val's table at lunch, or be nice to Gordie when he tries to say hello to me in the hall. Thank goodness I don't give into those drives. I'm usually okay if I take a couple of deep breaths and wait until they go away."

Sabrina rolled her eyes. Okay, so maybe Libby really *was* a jerk. But right now, she needed her.

"The thing I really want to know, Sabrina Spellman, is, *When are we going to wake up?* I'm being a pretty good sport about all this, but, to tell you the truth, I'm not sure how much more of it I can take!"

"I'm with you there!" Sabrina said. "But the fact is, you're about to wake up!"

"I am?" A look of such incredible relief

137

flashed across her features that Sabrina actually felt sorry for her.

"Yes. And all you have to do is come with me to the football field—right now!"

Libby raised her eyebrows. "Okay! But will I wake up in my own bed? Or will I wake up on the football field?"

"Does it matter?" Sabrina asked.

"No!" Libby answered. She looked ecstatic.

"Then let's go!"

"Let's go!" Libby echoed. The two girls took off like a double shot. Laughing and giggling, they raced each other back toward school, their feet pounding over the concrete, each one trying to be the first one there.

Chapter 13

"Hey everybody! Thanks for coming!"

The sky overhead was as blue as a robin's egg and birds and butterflies flew through the air or fluttered over the freshly cut grass of the football field. A few squirrels were having a great time dashing up the poles of the goal post and down again. Sabrina surveyed the faces around her, feeling happy. There was Val, her arms crossed over her chest, a let's-see-what-she's-going-to-do-now expression on her face. Gordie was wide-eyed, as if he didn't quite believe someone like Sabrina—who was the most popular cheerleader in the school, though not for too much longer, if she had her way—would actually have taken the time to talk to him. Harvey looked a little frustrated, though there was great love in his eyes.

And then there was Libby. She giggled, saying, "Boy, this is one dream I can't wait to wake up from!"

Cee Cee and Jill hadn't shown. *I guess shopping was more important to them than helping out a friend,* Sabrina decided. It didn't matter. Deep in her heart, she knew that all the important people were there, the people who could really help her get back in touch with herself.

But before she could do that, she had some explaining to do.

"All right," Val said. "Why are we here? Does everyone here have something to do with the food pantry?"

"Uh, not exactly," Sabrina said.

"Uh-huh! I knew it!" Val said. But she flopped onto the grass as she said it, which Sabrina took to mean that she was planning to stay rather than storm off.

"Food pantry? She told me we were going to be doing a science experiment," Gordie said. But he didn't seem to mind too much—maybe being close to Val was enough to satisfy him.

Harvey stepped over to Sabrina and held her gently by both shoulders. "You said you needed me. I thought you meant we were going to spend some time alone!" His voice was rich with passion.

Libby just giggled some more and said, "This dream gets weirder and weirder all the time!"

Even with all of them a little annoyed at her, Sabrina was glad to have them around her. She could already feel her old self slipping back inside her skin, like a foot into a comfortable shoe.

"Okay, listen people," she said. "It's true, I did get some of you here on false pretenses." There was a general grumbling, which Sabrina ignored. "The thing is, I need help—from all of you!" There, she'd said it—she needed her friends! She always had and she always would. And why not? "If you can't count on your friends," she said, "who can you count on?"

Val stared at her for a moment, then shook her head. "But Sabrina, we aren't friends!"

"Neither are we," Gordie said.

"Or us!" Libby agreed.

Sabrina heaved a deep sigh and sat down next to Val. The grass tickled the backs of her legs and the cheerleading uniform still itched. "Okay, okay. So right now, we're not. But maybe you could do me a favor and just *imagine* that we are. Pretend it's like, an alternate universe and I'm . . . I'm Libby here and Libby's me! She's the cheerleader, I'm the *Lantern* writer. What would we be doing then? Come on now. Help me out!" she pleaded.

For a moment there was silence, except for the songs of the birds. She hoped no one came out with a loud, "That's weird," or got up and left.

Thankfully, Harvey stepped in and smoothed

over the awkward moment. "Well, Sabrina, we *are* friends. More than friends. And if you weren't acting so bizarre, I'll tell you where we'd be . . ."

At the Slicery, Sabrina thought, *or home watching a rerun of last year's American High Schools Golf Tournament.*

"Under the bleachers, trying out some of the moves Brandon Bradley and Gladys Underwood did the other week!"

"Ooooh," Val squealed.

"Uh . . ." Gordie blushed.

"Wow, that would make some terrific gossip . . ." Libby murmured to herself.

Sabrina took Harvey's hand and gave it a loving squeeze. For an instant, she wished that all these people she'd gathered so painstakingly would just disappear for a moment so that she could throw her arms around him and give him a gigantic kiss. She resisted the urge to point them all over to the mall and turned her attention to Val. "So . . . what do you think? Can you humor me a little? What would we be doing if we were friends?"

Val shrugged. "I don't know. Maybe I'd be helping you with that *Lantern* story you mentioned. You know, we could both bring stuffed shopping bags to the food pantry. Maybe stop off at the bookstore on our way back from Ridgefield . . ."

Sabrina thought about it. It had been a great experience going to the food pantry on her own, but it would have been more fun with Val. Well, Kathleen had asked her to come back any time. Maybe next week, she and Val would go together. Next week, when things were back to normal again! She thought about the bookstore, too. She hadn't read much since she'd cast the switcheroo spell. It would be great to come home with a stack of books and get lost in some totally terrific story . . .

"Thanks, Val. That's really helpful." And it was. She turned to Gordie. "Okay, what about you?"

Gordie looked at her nervously, as if he were afraid she was going to bite his head off. "Well . . . if you were friends with Val, we'd probably all eat lunch together. And . . . and you wouldn't call me a freak anymore. And . . . you wouldn't interrupt my science experiments."

Sabrina nodded. "You're right. But Gordie, have you heard me call you a freak for . . . well, for the past week?"

He thought, staring up at the sky blankly. Then he said, "You're right, you haven't."

"See? We're already starting to be friends."

He tilted his head to one side. "I wouldn't go quite that far!"

Sabrina turned to Libby. "Okay. Last of all, let's hear from you! What would we be doing if you were me and I were you?"

Libby frowned, thinking. "Well, let's see . . . I'd probably insult you and call you a freak."

"Yeah, you probably would. Then what would happen?"

"Hmmm. I guess you'd try to say something clever to insult me back but I wouldn't particularly care because Cee Cee and Jill would be standing behind me giggling!"

"Right! And then?"

"I suppose then Mr. Kraft would come along and give you a big, fat detention slip."

"Yup, he probably would!"

Sabrina was in heaven. It was such a lousy scenario—and it all felt so wonderfully right! No matter what the negative points of her life, at the moment she would have given up winning the lottery to have them all back again! Maybe her life wasn't perfect, but it was hers. It reflected her choices, her needs, her friends—and she had to admit that she was pretty happy with it.

She closed her eyes, tuned in to herself and began to let Sabrina-like thoughts push out the bad Libby ones. *It's not how many friends you have, but how much you like them,* she thought. *It's not the number of parties you get invited to, but how fun they are. The world is full of magic, you just have to open your eyes and see it. There's no such thing as a freak, just someone who's made different choices than you. Cheerleading is not the most important activity at school. Niceness counts* . . . The thoughts kept coming. Friendly, positive ones. She realized as they flowed through her brain how much she'd missed them. Poor Libby—it was horrible thinking negatively.

At last, as the thoughts showed no sign of slowing down, she opened her eyes. Enough thinking—it was time for action! "Okay," she said, more to herself than to her friends. "I'm ready."

"Ready for what?" Gordie asked, but Sabrina didn't bother to answer.

She couldn't even remember how many good deeds she owed in order to switch back with Libby, so she just went crazy. Across the football field, a baby bird was just making its first feeble attempt to fly and failing miserably. Sabrina pointed and, *zooooooom*, off it soared. She remembered how bumpy some of the roads were in Westbridge. With a point of her finger they were all freshly paved. The local library was having a book drive, so with a magical gesture dozens of boxes filled with books appeared on the library's front steps. Another point of her finger and the town of Westbridge was suddenly giving out free passes to the local swimming pool. She conjured up nuts for the squirrels that chased up and down the goal posts and raised the temperature to exactly 72 degrees. *Point, point, point.* Parking meters were filled with coins; cars were instantly cleaned; dog pounds suddenly discovered lines of people outside their doors, just dying to adopt a stray.

Whoever said it's rude to point never met a witch! Sabrina giggled to herself.

Somewhere in the middle of her do-good frenzy, Sabrina wasn't exactly sure when, the air began to swirl and waver and shake. The sounds of the birds tweeting and the cars driving past the school building faded slightly. When the volume returned to normal and the whole world stabilized again, Sabrina realized that she was no longer wearing Libby's cheerleader outfit and that her own little blue-and-white striped dress hung comfortably from her shoulders. She'd done it! She'd reversed the spell!

She looked around the football field, at her friends, at the cars passing by. They all looked the same, yet everything was completely transformed! Still, she knew that when she got home today and told Aunt Hilda and Aunt Zelda what had happened, they'd be sure to ask her what she'd learned from the switcheroo experience. And if she didn't want to have to do dishes by hand for the rest of the school year, she better have a good answer ready.

She thought hard. What had she learned, really? *Hmmm,* she thought, *I learned that I don't particularly want to be the most popular girl in school. And that whatever I don't like about my*

*life, I'm still pretty happy with it. And I also
learned that doing good deeds is kind of fun.* Not
bad, she decided. She ought to be pointing up
clean dishes in no time!

She took one more look at Libby, the girl
whose life she'd lived for almost a week. Libby
was standing a little away from the others, scowling and scratching at the itchy fabric of the uniform. *Maybe that's why she's always in such a
bad mood,* she thought. *I mean, I know now how
awful it is to go around itching all day long.*

But in her heart of hearts, she knew it wasn't
the uniform. Libby just wasn't a very nice person. Now that she'd walked a week in her shoes,
she knew that for sure. Still, as she watched
Libby scratching and scowling, she couldn't help
feeling sorry for her.

Then she did one last good deed. She pointed
and Libby's frown melted first into a look of surprise, then into a smile. She stopped scratching.
That uniform would never make anyone itch
again!

About the Author

Margot Batrae lives and writes in New York City. She wrote *Switcheroo* on the back porch of her summer home in rural Massachusetts. She enjoys dancing, yoga, hiking, boating, and massive amounts of reading and writing of all kinds. As a child, Margot's favorite books and TV shows were about characters with magical powers or children who experienced magical adventures: the Edward Eager Half Magic Books, C. S. Lewis's Narnia Chronicles and, of course, Sabrina the Teenage Witch comic books! She is pleased to add her own vision of magic to the Sabrina series.

YOU AND A FRIEND COULD WIN A TRIP
TO THE KENNEDY SPACE CENTER
VISITOR COMPLEX TO SEE A REAL
SPACE SHUTTLE LAUNCH!

Sabrina
The Teenage
Witch

NO PURCHASE NECESSARY

1 Grand Prize: A 3 day/2 night trip for three (winner plus friend and a parent or legal guardian) to see a space shuttle launch at the Kennedy Space Center Visitor Complex in Florida. Prize also includes a Sabrina, The Teenage Witch CD-ROM, a Sabrina, The Teenage Witch hand held game, and a Sabrina, The Teenage Witch Diary Kit.

Alternate grand prize: In the event that the grand prize is unavailable, the following prize will be substituted: An Overnight Group Adventure at Apollo/Saturn V Center for three (winner plus friend and a parent or legal guardian). Winner and group will sleep under the Apollo/Saturn V rocket after an evening of space-related activities, including a Kennedy Space Center Visitor Complex group bus tour, pizza party dinner, a visit with Robot Scouts, hands-on activities. Winner and group will get a special NASA briefing of upcoming launches, demonstrations of Newton's Laws of Motion, midnight snack, breakfast and 3-D IMAX film. Prize includes a commemorative certificate for each group and patch for each participant.

10 First Prizes: A Sabrina, The Teenage Witch Book Library consisting of: Sabrina, The Teenage Witch, Showdown at the Mall, Good Switch, Bad Switch, Halloween Havoc, Santa's Little Helper, Ben There, Done That, All You Need is a Love Spell, Salem on Trial, A Dog's Life, Lotsa Luck, Prisoner of Cabin 13, All That Glitters, Go Fetch, Spying Eyes, Harvest Moon, Now You See Her, Now You Don't, Eight Spells a Week, I'll Zap Manhattan, Shamrock Shenanigans, The Age of Aquariums, Prom Time, Witchopoly, Bridal Bedlam, Scarabian Nights, While the Cat's Away, Fortune Cookie Fox, Haunts in the House, Up, Up and Away, Millennium Madness, Switcheroo, Sabrina Goes to Rome, Magic Handbook, and Down Under

20 Second Prizes: A Sabrina, The Teenage Witch gift package including a Sabrina, The Teenage Witch hand held game, a Sabrina, The Teenage Witch diary kit, and a Sabrina, The Teenage Witch CD-ROM

50 Third Prizes: A one-year Sabrina comic books subscription and a Sabrina, The Teenage Witch Diary Kit

---

Complete entry form and send to:
Pocket Books / "Sabrina, The Teenage Witch Space Launch Sweepstakes"
1230 Avenue of the Americas, 13th Floor, NY, NY 10020

NAME _____ BIRTHDATE ____/____/____

ADDRESS _____

CITY _____ STATE _____ ZIP _____

PHONE _____

See back for official rules

ARCHWAY
PAPERBACKS

VIACOM

KENNEDY SPACE CENTER
VISITOR COMPLEX

Pastime
#1 IN KIDS FUN!™

Knowledge Adventure
SABRINA SCHEDULE

TIGER
ELECTRONICS, LTD.